Dragon Tamers:
Reality Goes Virtual

By Emma Maree Urquhart

D1439921

ISBN 0-9549340-0-8

To my family.

4

Contents

The Dragon Tamer's Rulebook and Guide

The Dragon Tamer's Rulebook and Guide

Created by the Dragon Council

The Breaking of any of these rules will result in an instant
GAME OVER.

No apologies, no exceptions, no second chances.

This is a rulebook and Guide for the
'Dragon Tamers' Computer Game.

The Aim of the Game

In this game, you can have many different aims.
Some members aim to own the best looking valley, others the
strongest pet, to collect strange and powerful artefacts, to
look after their Dragon well and some players only
wish to end the game.
But whatever your aim, this book is essential reading if you want
to survive long enough to complete it.

Section 1 – Dragon Creation

When you join you are asked to create a Dragon.

To do this, there is a special programme, Dragon Creator X. There are different versions of this, you can use only one or can have access to all of them. They are: DCX Humanoid, Animal, Elemental and Specialist.

You can upload creations from one DCX to another, to create strange creatures like a dragon that specialises in speed with leopard colouring, or an animal with dragon wings.

You can use it to design and create your dragon in 3D form, and then test the finished dragon using training courses to see how it will move or perform tasks in Dragon Tamers. Then you can upload your finished creation onto the site.

When checked, dragons may be edited so they act properly in the game, or move easier, but this is rare and changes are minor. If you do not wish to have to wait for your dragon to be checked, you can use a preset design, and can change its basic features slightly.

Don't like any of the choices? Submit your own ideas to the Dragon Council, and they may be added to the next version of the program.

Section 2 – Dragon Elements

Each Dragon has his or her own element. These are:

Light – Dragons in charge of this element can change the amount of light in an area, can focus the sun's rays, and are particularly powerful when using fire magic and weapons.
These Dragons are usually: Kind creatures.

Dark - Dragons in charge of this element can change the amount of darkness in an area, can easily disappear into the shadows and

are particularly powerful when using black magic.
These Dragons are usually: Mean and cruel creatures.

Earth - Dragons in charge of this element can talk to animals,
cause plants to grow or die, can use nature's powers to their own
will and are particularly powerful when using natural weapons,
like sticks, stones, slingshots etc.
These Dragons are usually: Friendly animal lovers.

Water – Dragons in charge of this element often dwell in water and
also often have colouring to match the water which they love.
Common abilities for these dragons are communicating with fish,
walking on water or commanding the flow of it.
These Dragons are usually: Quiet, peaceful creatures.

Air – Dragons in charge of this element can control the flow of air,
and often their special ability is causing small hurricanes or
tornados.
They can communicate well with creatures of the air.
These Dragons are usually: Quiet, sad and withdrawn.

Fire - Dragons in charge of this element are able to cope with
extreme heat, like in the Dragon Realms volcanoes and often can
blow fire or summon it.
These Dragons are usually: Brave and bold, but fond of being in
control and hard to tame.

Electricity - Dragons in charge of this element can control electri-
cal currents and bolts of lightning.
These Dragons are usually: Friendly, but often sarcastic or snappy.

Section 3 – Dragons in Command of Special Powers

Some Dragons choose; instead of commanding an element, to
command other things.

Here are some of the most common choices.

Gravity – These Dragons can change the gravitational field.

Invisibility – These Dragons can disappear, but can still be smelled.

Healing – These Dragons have the power to heal the wounded.

Strength – These Dragons, usually covered in muscles, have great strength.

Defence – These Dragons, usually coated in armour, have great defensive powers.

Animation – These Dragons can turn inanimate objects into living, breathing things.

Magic – These Dragons specialise in using magic objects, casting spells etc.

The Gift of Tongues – These Dragons can speak in all languages.

Teleportation – These dragons can transport themselves and anybody else they wish to wherever they want to go.

Shape shifting: These Dragons can change into any shape or form that they wish.

Seetion 4 – Humanoids and Animal Types

Humanoids are Dragons that have been modelled on humans. They are weak creatures, and not favoured by other Dragons. However, they are very friendly, easy to tame Dragons.

The advantage in having these creatures is that they can stand on two legs, and are good at human skills like art and writing. With these Dragons, it is possible to have one that looks almost identical to you.

Animal types are an extremely common type of Dragon. They can look exactly like an animal, or can be altered versions of an animal. Despite trying to look like animals, they will often have some Dragon features, like a lizard tail, teeth or scales instead of fur.

Section 5 -The Planets

There are 10 planets, each with their own unique climate:

Tropica: The Tropical Planet, very little land, lots of water.

Frieze: The Cold Planet

Gael: The Windy Planet

Raze: The Hot Planet, not good for water dragons, but loved by fire dragons. It has a lot of volcanoes.

Serta: The Desert Planet

Sonok: The Water Planet. Not accessible.

Clix: The Starting Planet. Warm, with lots of plant life. It rains rarely, as the land does not need much moisture. When it does rain, the rainfall is quite low.

Berk: The Woodland Planet.

Dite: The Planet of Darkness and Touch Lights

Konica: This planet had never been visited, so there is no information about it.

Each planet also has their own Sun and Moon. All planets contain oxygen and gravity. All have rain every so often.
Above the beginners planet lays Destro, a planet only accessible using the 'Katapolt', a special object located on an island only accessible by winning a secret mini game.
This planet is guarded by Council Dragons and is only accessible to Tamers who have gotten into the Top 20 rank.

Section 6 - Battling

Dragons fight; it's their natural instinct to battle for their lives and their territory.
In this game, battles gain even more importance, with fighting wild dragons the only way to gain strength, and beating powerful bosses the only way to get further in the game.
Dragons always fight to the death, unless the opponent surrenders or both dragons have been instructed to do otherwise.
Because of the huge amount at risk, Dragons fight viciously. No blood is shed, as Dragons do not bleed.
A Dragon is not allowed to attack a tamer unless the tamer first attacks them. Attacking a defenceless tamer will result in the attacking dragon – or other wild creature – being deleted.
To keep the game fair when battling in groups, the strength of your enemies is tailored to suit you and your dragon's strength and how well you have battled before.

Section 7 – Items

Items can be found all around the site, or taken from defeated enemies.
These can be firewood, food for yourself or your dragon, items for

trading with other creatures or weapons (see Section 9).

At the beginning of the game, you will receive a rucksack containing a sleeping bag and a healing potion. These are embroidered with your username and a picture of your dragon, in case they are misplaced.

There is no limit to the amount of items you can put in your bag, but carrying a lot of items will lower your speed in the game.

All items in the bag are safe from water, fire, and many other things that happen in the game.

One of the bag's special features is the ability to disappear when not needed.

Section 8 – Signature Items

When you are beginning the game, you can create your own item, called your signature item.

As a weapon, it will be quite powerful, as battle items for the tamer are not common. Creating a weapon also comes in useful when your dragon is young, injured, or outnumbered. This is the most common choice.

However, the item does not have to be a weapon, or could even be an item disguised as something else. It is unique to you, and cannot be discarded, traded or sold.

This will gain more power, gain more features and become easier to use as your power increases in the game. These items void the rule that Dragons cannot harm humans, so if you use it during a battle you can be harmed.

Section 9 – Weapons and Spells

Weapons of many kinds are available in the game. These include guns, swords, poles, wands, bats, shields, cannons and more! They are found randomly around the site or taken from defeated enemies.

Also in the game, there are some powerful items that use magic spells. To use these, you need code words found around the site. If you have none of these items, these words can be traded with users for items or useful information!

Section 10 – Other Tamers

Other tamers play a large part in the game. Dragons can be instructed to fight each other or work alongside each other in teams. You can also trade spells, weapons and other items with other tamers. Keep a note of any tamers you are particularly friendly with. You may need their help before the end.

Section 11 – Other Creatures

Dragons are not the only creatures that inhabit this world. Some, like the Phoenix, are friendly, peaceful creatures, but others, like the Yeti, will attack as soon as they see you.
Here are some of the animals you will find -

The Kelpie – A green horse with seaweed for a mane. Found near and under water.
Leprechaun – A green clothed elf. Must be defeated quickly, before they teleport themselves to another area.
Pixies – These little creatures will nip and bite your Dragon constantly. They are tricky to hit due to their small size.
Minotaur – Found in the first few mazes, this Dragon look similar to a bull, with hooves and horns, but is actually a special breed of Dragon, with claws for hands and a long snout.
Troll – These big, strong creatures will hit your Dragon incessantly. However, it has no armour and the skin can be pierced by a Dragons claws. Also, it is a very unintelligent creature.
Unicorn – Dragons must keep away from this creature's sharp

horn, as it is capable of going straight through a Dragon's scales. They usually travel in groups.

Section 12 – The Snake

In this game, you play as 'The Chosen One', the one destined to save the world from the Destroyer.

But there is another character you may come across, the 'Snake', a player who pretends to be something he or she is not and will only lead you off the path. His or her actions can drastically affect how far you reach in the game and can even change the ending. This character is also rumoured to be under the control of the Destroyer.

Section 13 – The Plot

At the start of the game, you are told the story of the game. As it progresses, you are told even more about it. Here is the first Section in the story, in case you have forgotten it.

Part 1 – The Start of the Game

The sun is setting upon the land of the Dragons, night is drawing near. Nestled underneath a bush lies a Dragon's egg, alone and destined to die soon. Suddenly, you appear beside it.

It is your destiny to raise this egg and tame the Dragon inside it. Go now and complete you task!

Part 2 – After your Dragon becomes an adult

That night, while you sleep, a great many battles are fought. Something came in the night, killing every dragon in the area.

All apart from yours. Hidden in the valley, you were not found.
Now you have a quest. You must find out who killed them all.
Pack your items and get ready for the journey. You may need a lot
of food, why not catch some fish down by the pond outside the
valley.

Part 3 – When the player returns from the pond

When you were out fishing, a great storm tore through your valley, destroying your home. But wait a minute…if it was a storm,
why is nothing wet with rain? And how come the storm didn't
reach out by the pond?
When you arrive home and find deep claw marks gouged into the
walls, you finally realise it was the 'Destroyer', the monster
which had killed all the other Dragons. And if you had not gone
fishing, it would have gotten you and your Dragon as well.
It's no longer safe in the valley, so go out and find the creature
that did this, and defeat the mysterious monster that is destroying
your world!

End of the First Level of the Game

Sometimes, things done in the game will affect the plot and start a
side quest or alternative plot.
Also included in the main plot are mini games to play for prizes
or for fun.

Section 14 – The Destroyer

Not much is known about the monster known as the Destroyer.
The Snake is forced to work for him, if he did not he or she would
be killed. For now, the Destroyer spares his/her life.
The Destroyer (we assume he is male) has a huge amount of
power, and can destroy almost anything. He has no known weak-

ness. No player has won in a battle against the Destroyer, and all who lose receive an instant Game Over.

Section 15 – Cheats, Scams and Hacks

Cheats and hacks, or outside programmes of any kind are not allowed in this game and the using of these will result in an immediate game over.
This includes: Programs, Refreshers, and anything else which makes the game unfair for other players. Breaking this rule WILL get your account deleted.

Section 16 – The Player's Promise

Not sure if a player is telling the truth? To make sure no one makes false promises in the game, there is a rule called 'The Player's Promise'. If any player makes this promise and what they say is not true, they will receive a Game Over.

Section 17 - Leaving the Game

Dotted throughout the level are healing shrines, a place to heal and rest. These places are also save spots, and if you quit the game you will restart at the last shrine you visited. They are often hidden; try asking the areas inhabitants if they know of any nearby.

Section 18 – Things that will get you an immediate Game Over

There are many things in this game which will result in a game over. Here is a list of some of them.

Losing a battle against the destroyer.
Knowingly using other user's artwork for creating
your own Dragon.
Failing to tame you Dragon, causing it to go wild.
Using Programmes.
Scamming other users.
Hacking into other users accounts.
Taking advantage of other users.
Attacking a user's dragon who doesn't want to battle.
Attacking a user on purpose (sometimes a Dragon may hit you by
accident, like if a burst of flame misses its target) when they don't
have a weapon.
Pretending to be a member of the council
Pretending to be another player.
Breaking a Player's Promise.

Avoid doing all of these things and you might even
complete the game!
Good luck!

The Dragon Council

$Chapter$ 1 : *Aboard the Wave Rider*

Caroline O'Nearn sat on the top deck of the *Wave Rider,* her dad's boat, staring out at the wide blue ocean, stretching for miles in front of her.

Once a year, during the summer, Carol would have to join her parents on a cruise to places ranging from the cold, windy cliffs of Scotland's highlands to the sun and heat of Spain, all in their huge cruise ship.

The ship was very popular, containing some of the most advanced technology in the world. Its most popular attraction was a cinema with seats that moved or vibrated along with the movie. It also had gourmet foods, a swimming pool, five star bedrooms and much more.

Despite all this, Carol often found herself quite bored. She knew every part of the ship, and had bases in most of them, where she would sneak away from her dreaded tutor and play games on her laptop. Today, she was sitting behind some rope at the front of the ship playing her laptop on battery power.

She was playing a game called *Dragon Tamers*. It was the only thing she used the laptop for, apart from finding information about the game on the Internet.

The actual Creator of the game had never been seen by players, and his identity in the real world was only known by the companies who worked with him. He had been on the news recently, because he had been missing for a long time. They still hadn't said what he looked like, but there were rumours that he was not an adult, but a teenager.

In *Dragon Tamers* you played a young girl or boy who had appeared long ago in the mythical Dragon Realm, with a dragon's egg sitting beside you.

The aim of the game was to look after your dragon until he or she was nearly an adult, at which point the game's plot started, with a mysterious creature slaughtering all the wild dragons in the area. The player then found that he had to save the rest of the dragons. You were, of course, given the choice of hiding, but as the unknown destroyer rampaged the lands, the player found the valley was no longer safe as the dragon's home was mysteriously destroyed while both player and partner were out catching fish, the main food source at a pond outside the valley.

Then the player set out on his quest filled journey to defeat the destroyer, a task that no one had yet completed.

Unlike your usual battle, where if you lost a match your dragon would be reborn, players who had been defeated by the destroyer received an immediate game over and were not allowed back to the Dragon Realm.

The only way you had of gaining power was by destroying other creatures as when killed, all the loser's strengths and powers would belong to the winner.

This, to Carol, was life. To her the game was real, and her dragon (which, like all others, was unique to the player) was called Samantha, or Sam, and was a beautiful water living female dragon, with long webbed hands and feet and coloured, scaly wings. Her grey-blue body made her almost invisible in the dark water.

She would glide effortlessly, wings outstretched, through the water. Her long neck stretched out for metres in front of her body, ending in her head, with its large, soft brown eyes and odd, bottle like nose and mouth and nostrils that could close, at which time she would open some gills hidden behind her ears, letting her breath under water. When she came out of the water again her gills would close and nostrils open, allowing her to live on any terrain. Her head ended in two dark blue horns, slight curved and ending in two cruel points.

Most people would be terrified by Sam, but not Maree (Carol's game name), the tamer of that noble creature.

Often Carol yearned to be more like Maree, with her short, bobbed black hair, long, thin fingered hands and adventurous life, instead of boring Carol, with a short, chubby build, ginger hair, pale skin (from always sitting in front of the computer screen) that never tanned and ever repeating life.

20

At first, Carol had been a fit, sport loving girl, but when she had found out about the Dragon Tamers game, her life had gradually faded away until only one important thing remained, the game. Her only friends were the ones she had online, Dragon Tamer addicts like her. She had even become afraid of finishing the game, she started to stay in one area and train instead of following the plot. That was how she had become the strongest player in the game. In the real world, her only thoughts were of the game, and she often daydreamed the day away about it, and was always scolded for having her 'head in the clouds' all day long and never paying attention to what was happening in the real world, resulting in continual bumping into things, and overall clumsiness.

Perhaps that is what brought about the next event. No one knows for certain, but most people believe that it was something different.... much different

*   *   *

It happened on the tenth day of the trip. It was hot and humid, and the cruise passengers were restless, so her dad had gone down to provide entertainment, while her mum was ever busy in the kitchen, preparing food.

Carol was wandering aimlessly around the ship. She had been told not to use the computer that day, to give her eyes a rest (and her head, too). Carol hated being banned from using the laptop, but she was terrified of having to wear glasses, so obeyed her parents. She wandered down to the outdoor swimming pool, and climbed down a ladder behind it to the 'crew only' area, which, of course, she was allowed in.

It was empty. Carol went and sat by the railing, sitting on the rails that scuba divers used to jump off.

She had thought that she might get to go for a swim in the sea, but at a glance she saw it would be impossible. The boat was going too fast for anyone to swim alongside and she would get dragged down by the current.

Last night, she had charged her laptop and hidden it here. Now, she took it out and, making sure her parents couldn't see, started playing the game.

She watched Sam gliding through the pond's dark waters, with Maree, able to breath under water while sitting on Sam, recording it to use as a screensaver.

Like all dragons, Sam had her own special element, water, which she was able to control. One of the abilities of commanding the water element was that she was able to let her tamer breath under water. Also, she had gained the ability of breathing lightning, which she used in battle and to cook food.

Sam was a champion among dragons, and Maree was a champion tamer. Every game player knew of them. Carol was glad that every dragon was different; she wouldn't be able to bear it if there was another Sam.

As she sat on the boat, she could almost see Sam's long neck gliding through the water, which looked very similar to the water flowing below her. It was amazingly realistic. She turned the laptop's volume up to full, and plugged in her earphones. She always did that when playing. The game had no music; only the sound of the Dragon Realm and with her earphones in, the game world seemed to be all around her.

With the sounds blaring in her ears, Carol failed to hear her pet Labrador, Rogue, jump down some crates of supplies and run up behind her, ready for a game. The excited dog ran straight at her, waiting for Carol to move out of the way and grab at him before he fell off the side, which was what usually happened, resulting in a tangle of dog and human. But Carol didn't notice the dog, intensely staring at the screen. The dog ran straight into her, sending Carol, along with her laptop, tumbling down into the water.

For what seemed like hours, but was more likely only seconds, Carol paddled furiously, trying to stay on top of the water, crying out for help, but instead receiving a mouthful of water. Her laptop had already sunk like a stone to the bottom.

Finally, Carol's mum came out to see what was causing Rogue's incessant barking, but when she got there, Carol had already been pulled under by the currents caused by the boat, and, unable to swim against it any longer, had sank down into the bottomless depths of the sea.

Chapter 2: *The Dragon Realm*

Under the surging waves, as Carol's limp body sank, a strange thing happened.

The sea seemed to glow, and a bolt of lightning surged through Carol's unconscious mind, awakening it. But what her eyes saw was not a tunnel of bright light, blue water, or a sunny sky, but a whirl of bright colours, spinning before Carol's face. She seemed to be flying. Her feet were motionless, the world around her was unchanging, yet Carol was sure she was moving.

Then, the colours faded, and Carol found herself lying face down on a grass bank. Sitting up, she found she was dry and unhurt. The world around her seemed familiar. She must have seen it while sitting out on deck.

She was wearing a different pair of shoes, made from the same material as her V.R. suit, and she was covered in a thick cloak, black to match the rest of her clothes. Oddly enough, it looked exactly like the clothes she wore in the *Dragon Tamers* game!

She was worried. There was no sign of a living person anywhere, or the sea. Also, the ground was littered with the bones of animals, or at least, Carol *hoped* they were the bones of *animals*.

Behind her lay a pond. It was dark and deep, with strange fish swimming around in it.

Then she saw something that made her blood run cold. In front of her, viciously attacking a smaller one of its specie was a dragon. And not just any dragon. It was Samantha.

*   *   *

Carol watched, her fear growing with every second, as Sam viciously tore at her opponent. No blood fell. Dragons don't bleed. She sat frozen to the spot as Sam fired a deadly bolt of lightning at the opponent, and it exploded in a pile of purple dust, which Sam greedily ate, absorbing the entire dragon's power into herself.

Carol thought about running. She couldn't. Even if she could summon up the courage to, the dragon could run more than ten times faster than her. Sam sniffed the air, tense after the battle.

Sam turned towards her, brown eyes gazing curiously at Carol, as it started walking towards her, and Carol hurriedly crawled backwards. The dragon cocked its head to one side and took a couple more steps forward. Carol uttered a frightened squeak, and tried again to crawl away, but found that her exit was blocked by a small cave, in which lay Sam's bed, a pile of grass, moss and leaves. She had crawled into a dead end, with a dragon in front of her and a stone wall on all other sides. With nowhere to run, she closed her eyes and waited to die.

But instead, the dragon stepped nimbly around her and lay down in the middle of its bed and began chewing on a bone. Then it looked up, gave a huge yawn, showing rows of pointed teeth, and started speaking.

"Maree, what's gotten into you? You look scared to death."

For a minute, Carol just stared, in shock. Then the dragon laughed. "Oh, I nearly forgot, you just got here! Sorry, I've been rather busy, and as you've been here since last night, you kind of became part of everything...Well, you know what I mean."

"Actually, I don't. Where am I?"

"You're in the Dragon Realm! Surely you can't have forgotten!"

"I'm in a computer game?"

"Let me explain. The Destroyer has been destroying the entire Dragon Realm and all the dragons agreed that we needed help. So, we called in our toughest player, by combining all our magic and transporting the player here from the real world."

Then what she had to do began to slowly sink in.

"You mean... *I* have to save the dragon realm!"

"Yes. With my help."

"But...I'm not a fighting person! The sight of blood makes me faint! I bruise   easily!" Remembering Sam's battle with the intruder, Maree couldn't help herself from shivering.

"You were a fighting person when you were playing the game."

24

"But I'm not playing the game! If I was, everything wouldn't seem so real!"

"Well that's why it's called virtual *reality*. It's meant to seem real. And while you're playing, it is. You are Maree, the strongest player in the game."

"But I don't want to do this! I want to go home!" Cried Maree. "I want to be Carol again!"

"Well...there's a problem," said Sam, scratching the ground nervously with her back feet. "You can't. The game was shut down after you arrived. You can only get back if you finish the game."

"How many chances do I get?" Asked Maree. Surely she'd be able to have extra lives!

"One. But sleeping in safe areas will help you to heal."

"*Great*. What happens if I lose?"

"You die. And it's game over for all the dragons in the realm."

"If I die, will I get back home?"

"No. For you, everything that happens is real, not part of the game. And if you die in the game, you'll be dead in the real world, and it will be just as painful."

That said, Sam began to curl up, ready for a sleep. Looking out, Maree saw that it had become dark.

Sam yawned and shot a bolt of lightning at some grass and twigs in the corner starting a fire which roared away happily in the small dip in the cave it had been place in, with rocks and earth packed tightly around it to stop it spreading across the grass covered cave floor.

There was time in the Realm, based on Greenwich Mean Time, but many members didn't use it, and relied on the position of the sun or moon in the sky. Most members only slept when they needed to save, but Maree wasn't just playing the game like she normally would. She felt tired.

With a defeated sigh, she curled up in the corner of the room and slowly drifted into a dreamless, uneasy sleep.

*   *   *

In a different valley…

She was trotting along a field, on her horse. It was getting dark, she should turn back before she reached the woods. Her horse paused, tensing.

"There's something there…" She whispered, trying to look through the trees and see what. There was a rustling, and something appeared.

Her horse reared up, and she was thrown into the air before she could see what it was. After that, all she could remember was darkness…

"I don't understand! Why hasn't she left the game with the other players?" said someone, waking her.

Hushed voices, more talking. Who was it?

"But this wasn't supposed to happen! She only just joined! I don't care if you went to the trouble of forwarding time so she wouldn't have to raise me first!"

The yelling stopped, and there was the sound of beating wings.

"It's not fair! Why me?" The second voice said, snorting angrily.

"What's wrong?" the girl asked, brushing her blond hair from her eyes and looking round.

"Ellen…You're awake?"

"No, I'm dreaming. That's why my horse is talking." Ellen said groggily, staring at the winged horse standing in front of her.

"No, you're playing a computer game. You only just joined. I'm your dragon, Crystal."

"That confusing RPG thing? I thought I logged out hours ago, and went riding! I need to go."

"I'm afraid you can't." Crystal said slowly.

"What? Why not?"

"You're stuck in the game for a while. You can't log out."

"Why? I need to get home!"

"You can't. This is your home for now."

"There has to be a way out! This is just a computer game!"

"Where are you going? That way leads to the maze! Wait, stop!"

Chapter 3: *The Shadow in the Night*

That night, the Destroyer killed more. Its cruel weapons ripped
open its victim's bodies, without even giving them a chance to
fight.

Tonight was special. They had come here not just to slaughter, but
to watch.

In the darkness, a shadow lurked, commanding its monster. His
face was hidden by the darkness, but he seemed to be male.
During the fight, he would inspect the Dragon carefully. Then he
would either leave it to be blown away by the wind, or collect it in
a clear plastic container and give it to the Destroyer. Hiding in the
shadows, he watched Maree as she slept. But he didn't do anything. At least, not yet.

*   *   *

Maree was woken the next morning by the sound of whispered
conversation. Trying not to be noticed, she opened an eye and saw
Sam, reading a piece of parchment, a smaller dragon by her side,
nervously watching Sam. It was a Kilimario, or dragon messenger.
Kilimario are specially designed characters, small and thin, with a
streamlined body and large wings enabling them to go faster than
any bird on Earth.

Their only role in the game was to deliver message scrolls from
player to player.

Sam seemed startled by the news. She was talking quickly and
firmly, puffs of smoke and zaps of electricity issued between
words.

"Maree, you might want to read this for yourself, instead of
watching me read it." she said, without even turning her head.
"Okay" said Maree, startled at the acuteness of the Dragon's senses.
Sam handed her a small piece of parchment.

Dear Sam and Maree

We regret to inform you that some younger members
of our community
have stolen some dragon dust from stores and used it to summon
more humans into the realm, the second strongest player, and,
accidentally, a new player who was joining at the same time the
spell was cast, in an attempt to
save the realm themselves.
Player Ceirin, the 2nd strongest, has gone ahead to clear
his area of foes,
but beginner Ellen has trapped herself in the Labyrinth, normal
difficulty, and can't get out.
As the only human around the area, it would be great
if you could go rescue her.
Many thanks

The Dragon Council

"Tell them we'll be right over," said Maree to the Kilimario,
sighing. She couldn't help getting annoyed by new tamers. Getting
stuck in the first Labyrinth!
"Come on Sam, before the Minotaur gets her."

Chapter 4: *Labyrinth of the Minotaur*

"Help! Somebody! Anybody!" Ellen's cries rang through the labyrinth as the Minotaur, a bull type dragon (dragons sometimes resemble animals, at which point they are known as 'types' of dragons) that challenged players who entered the maze and could only be beaten by a certain form of weapon, which was why the maze was an optional area to visit. Ellen didn't have that weapon. In fact, she had no weapon.

As Maree flew down, she could see the girl charging through the maze on her horse-type winged dragon. This would be too easy. "Fly out of range" she yelled down, pulling a sword hilt out of a sheath on her side. Then the weapon started glowing purple, and it became clear that there was an actual sword, but it was invisible.

As the player flew up, Maree swooped down in front of the charging creature. Concentration was the key. Just as it reached her, out came her sword, which was driven right through the creature. It disappeared in a cloud of dust.

Then Sam gulped down the dust. Ellen looked shocked.

"You...you...killed it!" she said.

"Of course I did. You need to eat Dragon Dust to get stronger. Anyway, don't worry, wild dragons don't really die; they get reborn, didn't you read the manual? This one will be reborn into a new Minotaur. Harden up, Ellen. This is the dragon realm. Dragons aren't cuddly, fluffy creatures. They're scaly hunting machines, designed to fight." Maree said. She hadn't meant to be so harsh, but she had seen players like Ellen before, and they annoyed her.

"I don't know if I agree with you there..." Murmured Sam to herself.

"But couldn't you just talk to it?" sobbed Ellen. Maree groaned. A complete newbie and an idiot to boot.

"It's not her fault, Maree," coaxed Sam. "She's stuck in the game that she doesn't even know how to play. It's all new to her."

Maree looked at Ellen for the first time. She was wearing a jockey's outfit, but made differently to normal outfits. It was a dark material that fluttered softly in the breeze. As nice as it looked, the material was thin and wouldn't be very good at keeping her warm. Her hair was blonde, and tied up in, ironically, a pony tail.

Her dragon was quite an amazing creature. Its hooves were pure dragon crystal, her wings were tipped with crystal spikes similar to the clear, shining horn sat upon her head. A grey mane hung loosely over her face, and it's body sparkled in the light, suggesting scales instead of hair.

"Come on, let's get out of here," said Maree, walking back to the fishing pond.

"What happened? How did I get here?" asked Ellen.

"Yes, how did we get here even though the game's down?" Crystal asked. "Ellen had just hatched me when she was evacuated from the game."

"Well, there's trouble here, and two of us were called into the game. Then a dragon tried to bring some more players, but the spell went wrong and you ended up here," explained Maree.

"We have to look after the humans" Sam added, to Crystal.

"I know. I tried explaining things to her, but she didn't listen."

"But I only bought the game yesterday! I haven't even played it yet; all I did was create a Dragon and a costume. I was taken out of the game a few minutes after I started! I went out horse riding, and somehow I ended up in the game."

"That is pretty strange...I was playing the game when it happened to me. I wonder if that happened to the other player. Look, why don't you stay in my valley for the night, and tomorrow we'll try to figure out what to do with you."

"Stay? Why can't I just logout of the game?" Ellen asked, confused.

"You can't go home. We're both stuck here for a while," Maree replied.

"There's plenty of time left. I should find my own cave again; I think I remember where it was. I'll see you tomorrow, perhaps," Said Ellen, seeming shocked.

Maree hesitated before letting her go. Something didn't feel right. Then she remembered that nothing happened to a new player on his or her first few days. She'd be safe. Reluctantly, she watched Ellen leave, and then headed back to her own home.

When they arrived, another messenger was waiting. She grabbed the scroll and stuffed it into her pocket. It could wait.

"Don't you think you should read that?" asked Sam.

"No. It's probably another newbie in trouble. It can wait until the morning. I'm tired. Goodnight Sam. Don't let the Dragons bite!" Maree yawned, curling up in the cave corner.

"It's still the afternoon," Sam replied.

"Then we'll go swimming and catch some fish," Maree said, getting up again. They spent most of that day at the large pond, swimming underwater, catching fish, and generally having fun. She had enjoyed swimming in the game, but it was even better now she was in the game world.

Eventually, when the sun started to go down, they returned to the cave. Sam lit a fire, scaled and gutted the fish with her own claws, out of sight of Maree, then brought the meat back and Maree cooked it. Maree had not been here for long, but already she was beginning to accept the fact that she would be for a while.

After their meal, they settled down for yet another sleep, now actually tired.

Not long after they'd both fallen asleep, a scream echoed throughout the valley.

* * *

Maree. Where are you? Something's wrong! I need help! I don't know where you are. Danger!
Ellen? What's wrong? Where are you?
They're coming! They're in the valley!
Ellen? Ellen!

* * *

31

"Ellen? Ellen? Speak to me..." Two claws grabbed her shoulder, shaking her roughly.

"Are you OK? I think you were having a nightmare," said Sam.

"No," said Maree, now wide awake. "Something's wrong. Nightmares aren't part of the game...Where's the message I was sent?"

"In your pocket, why?" Sam was confused. Maree hurriedly unrolled it and started reading:

Dear Sam and Maree

We apologize for using your time, but you must not, at all costs, let Ellen and her dragon Crystal out of your sight. As a weak player, she is in great danger. Keep her with you.

The Dragon Council

Maree paled. If this message arrived last night, she might already be too late.

Chapter 5: *The Snake*

Sam tracked Ellen's trail through the network of valleys, most of them empty because the game was offline, until Maree and she reached the valley where she had stayed. One look made it clear that something bad had happened.

The ground had been trampled flat, and the cave walls had been scored by deep claw marks.

In one corner, a fire was slowly burning away. Beside it lay a riding cloak, stained with dark red blood.

"I'm sorry Maree," sighed Sam. "It looks like they are gone."

"No. They can't have been destroyed, only captured! I'm sure that, last night, Ellen found a way to contact me. When I was asleep, she managed to talk to me. We have to find her!"

"Her player status is normal, but her location is blocked. Did she tell you where she was?" Sam asked. All Dragons had a programme built into them that let them scan characters.

"No. She can't have gone that far. We'll just have to search until we find her."

*　　　*　　　*

"Maybe she's gone further than I thought..." said Maree, after an hour's searching.

"You've never left the first area, Clix. Maybe the instruction manual can give us some clues as to where she might be." Sam said, as Maree pulled the book from her bag. Maree had got to her rank by staying in the one area and fighting other dragons. The strength of opponents didn't change in different areas, but instead rose as Maree's did, so she never found the dragons in the Valley too weak.

"All right then, pass the manual..." The manual, or rulebook, was a special book given to all players, written by the Dragon Council, which contained the rules and other useful information about the game.

Section 5 -The Planets

There are 10 planets, each with their own unique climate:

Tropica: The Tropical Planet, very little land, lots of water.

Frieze: The Cold Planet

Gael: The Windy Planet

Raze: The Hot Planet, not good for water dragons, but loved by fire dragons. It has a lot of volcanoes.

Serta: The Desert Planet

Sonok: The Water Planet. Not accessible.

Clix: The Starting Planet. Warm, lots of plant life, rains rarely, as the land does not need much moisture. When it does rain, it is quite light.

Berk: The Woodland planet.

Dite: The Planet of Darkness and Touch Lights

Konica: This planet had never been visited, so there is no information about it.

Each planet also has their own Sun and Moon. All planets contain oxygen and gravity. All have rain every so often.
Above the beginners planet lays Destro, a planet only accessible using the 'Katapolt', a special object located on an island only accessible by winning a secret mini game.
This planet is guarded by Council Dragons and is only accessible to Tamers who have gotten into the Top 20 rank.

"Maybe she's been taken to Destro..." suggested Sam.

"Don't tell me. This is going to turn into one of those big quests, isn't it" said Maree.

"I couldn't possibly tell," said Sam with a grin. Certain things in the game activated alternate plots or side quest, and this looked like one of them, It was always much more fun taking part in a plot no one else was part of. Just as she was thinking about this, she heard a voice.

"Psst! Sam! Maree!" whispered the Voice.

"What the- who's there?" asked Maree.

"Ceirin," whispered Ceirin. He was sitting crouched underneath a tree, his Dragon, a shape shifter, sitting on his shoulder in lizard form.

"What are you doing here?" whispered Maree, though she didn't know why. There was no one around.

"The trees have ears. Come to my cave," he said, heading towards a flight of steps a short walk away. He was a boy of about 13, with black hair and dark brown eyes. He walked slowly and carefully, as if the ground might crumble away at any moment. His Dragon circled high above, as a peregrine falcon, searching the ground below.

"Talk about paranoia!" whispered Maree to Sam.

He reached the steps and climbed down. Maree and Sam followed him. It led into a cave, floored and furnished. Ceirin had obviously spent a lot of time playing the game before he was transported there.

"What's so important that we had to go all the way down here to hear it?"

"I've found out some vital information about the Destroyer. If we use it correctly, we might be able to destroy it."

"Great. Tell us, Ceirin!"

"Well, you'll know from the manual that above this planet lies the planet Destro, the most likely place for the Destroyer to hide. It can be reached using the Katapolt, which lies on an island around here somewhere. I've managed to find out the Mini Game we need to complete to find out which island."

"If it's a planet, why can't we see it?" Sam asked.

"'Planet' is just a name for all the different areas. In fact, they're all connected like countries, and can be entered simply by stepping over a border. Destro is different, it's a floating island above the main planets."

"So what's the Mini Game called?" asked Maree.

"It's called 'Riddle of the Sphinx', it's a puzzle game, located in the desert planet."

"Serta. I've heard of it," Maree said, nodding. "Not good for battling, the Mini Games the only interesting thing there."

"Have you ever actually played it?"

"No. We didn't travel far," Sam replied.

"We better set off. Can Nick carry you by air?" Maree asked. Nick nodded.

"Maree," said Sam, "What about Ellen?" Maree frowned. In all the excitement, she had forgotten about Ellan.

"Ellen? The new player?" asked Ceirin.

"Yes, she was captured by the Destroyer not long ago. We have to find her."

"I knew it!" shouted Ceirin, shocking Maree and Sam.

"Knew...what...?" asked Maree.

"Don't you see? It's so obvious! The rulebook and guide talks of a 'Snake', a player under the control of the Destroyer, who will lead you to your doom!" cried Ceirin, pulling out his rulebook.

"But it can't be Ellen...she's just a newbie! And the Destroyer tried to kill her!"

"Think about it. It all makes sense. What is there to say she's just a newbie? And was it just an odd coincidence that she got transported here with us? And how come she wasn't destroyed by the Destroyer? Answer: She's under his control!"

"He has a point. The Destroyer's never harmed a player before, either, only the wild Dragons."

"No...No...You're wrong...All wrong..." said Maree, shocked. When they had met, Maree and Ellen had connected, no matter how hard she had tried to hide it. Maree pitied the newbie, and wanted to help her get started, though she hid it well. She wanted

36

to give Ellen the help she never got when she first entered the game...even when she really needed it...

"Maree..." said Ceirin softly, "She's a spy...a deceiver!"

"No..." repeated Maree, backing away. This was wrong. She ran out of the cave, into the forest. Ellen couldn't be the deceiver, she had sounded so sad and helpless when she had contacted Maree...

Ceirin appeared beside her. His Dragon wasn't with him.

"Maree," he said, his voice soft, "I'm sorry. I wish I wasn't the one to tell you that..."

"I don't believe you. She's just an innocent player. She isn't even meant to be in this game, her dragon's a lot weaker than ours."

"Look, we only just met. I don't want us not to be friends just because of this. It's just what I think. If you don't believe me, then you don't have to."

Ceirin was right. It was stupid, falling out over this.

"Maree, I'm going to fight the Destroyer, and I want you to come with me..." As he said this, Maree remembered something. The same words...

"Maree," he had said, "I have to go and fight the Destroyer, and I want you to come with me,"

"No!" she had cried, "You're not strong enough to fight him! I don't want to lose you!"

"If you won't come with me, then I must go alone..." He had looked sad...

"Fine then! Go get yourself killed!" Oh, how she regretted those words, perhaps if she had never said them....

"What's with you?" He asked, also angry. "What are you afraid of?"

"I'm not afraid of anything!"

"You never leave the valley!"

"Why should I? To get a game over?"

"There's no point! How can we be brave if we never face our fears?"

He had leapt onto the Katapolt, and was thrown into the air, his Dragon following him; she didn't remember what it looked like.

37

*They had been the best of friends, but her fears for Sam had
caused them to fall out and be separated.*
*The next day, Maree had checked his player status. There was
none, it had all been erased from the game. He had gotten a game
over...*

"We're the two top players. If anyone can beat this game, it's us."
Ceirin finished.
Maree stood there, staring at this boy, she realised he actually
looked quite like her old friend. It wasn't his fault, probably just a
coincidence. But it was strange.
"If you're going after the Destroyer, then I'm coming with you,"
said Maree. No matter how much she feared for Sam, no matter
how much she wanted to stay here where it was safe, she was
going to beat the game, and nothing was going to stop her.

Chapter 6: *Riddle of the Sphinx*

"So how many islands are there, anyway?" asked Maree, flying on Sam's back.

"According to this, loads, but only a few big enough for the Katapolt." Said Ceirin, looking at something while sitting on Nick, who was flying in the form of a large albatross.

"What is that?" Maree asked, looking at Ceirin.

"It's a game map. I get Nick, my Dragon, to fly up as high as he can and tell me what he sees. I draw what he tells me on this."

"I meant, what's that computer?"

"It's a P.D.A. I was given it when I started."

"Who by?"

"I don't know. It was just there in my starter pack." Ceirin replied, shrugging.

"So, how do we play this Mini Game? You seem to know a lot about it."

"I used to own a fan site for Dragon Tamers, that's how I know so much about it. There was a large group of players who would help each other out in the forums. It's a mini-game, played on the desert planet. You have to answer loads of riddles, and each correct answer gets you a clue. But if your answer is wrong, you have to battle, and the Sphinxes are pretty strong…"

"Well, we don't have much choice." Maree said, shrugging, and they flew straight towards Serta, with Ceirin telling them where to go.

*   *   *

An hour later, they landed in the middle of the Desert. Well, they thought that was the middle of the Desert. It was hard to tell with all the sand flying everywhere.

"How are we meant to find a Sphinx in this?" said Nick, spitting out mouthfuls of sand and transforming into a llama, then correcting himself and turning into a camel.

"Trust me, they're pretty hard to miss!" shouted Ceirin over the roaring wind. And he was right!

The Sphinx was the size of a mountain, carved out of sandy coloured rock that seemed to flow like water, giving the Sphinx complete freedom of movement. It had the body of a lion, with sand all over it. Gradually, the fur patterns became skin and instead of a lion's head it had a woman's head, shoulders and arms, giving it four feet and a pair of arms. Flames burst from its nostrils and instead of human molars it had row upon row of sharp teeth, like that of a shark. And the worst part? There were ten of them, there huge bulk blocking the sandstorm, creating a calm area for the questioning to happen.

Apart from the Sphinx, there was nothing unusual about the desert. There were some palm trees, an Oasis around which the Sphinx gathered, and of course, a lot of sand.

"So we have to answer *ten* riddles?" questioned Ceirin.

"Yes. That's the thing with mini games. They're hard." said Sam.

"Then why don't they change them? Mini Games aren't always like puzzles; they can be fun things like skating and surfing!"

"I have no idea why you're asking *me* that." said Sam.

"STEP FORWARD!" boomed the first sphinx.

"Solve this riddle, and you may pass,

But if you are incorrect, that word will be your last!" The sphinx grinned, its teeth shining in the light of the sun.

"I am in a cave, but I am always wet. What am I?"

"Ummmmmm....." said Maree, pondering the question. "Any suggestions, Ceirin?"

Ceirin ignored her, too busy staring, awe-struck, at the sphinx.

"Wow....Look at those teeth...."

"Teeth?" said Maree. They were trying to solve a riddle, and he was busy looking at teeth! Boys...

"I must take your first answer!" cried the Sphinx.

40

"Huh? Wait! That wasn't my answer! I didn't mean to say-"
"TEETH IS….CORRECT! MOVE ONTO THE NEXT SPHINX!"
boomed Sphinx One.
"Phew…" said Maree, "That's what I call lucky! But wait, what
about my clue?"
"You are headed for planet Destro, above the planet of Clix." said
Sphinx one.
"That's the clue? It's written in the instruction manual!" said Nick
angrily.
"STEP FORWARD!" boomed the second Sphinx.
"Solve this riddle, and you may pass,
But if you are incorrect, that word will be your last!"

*"In the morning, I walk on four legs, in the afternoon on two, and
in the evening on three. What am I?"*

"Easy," said Maree under her breath. This riddle was older than
she was!
"You are a human, on four legs as a baby, two as an adult and with
stick in old age."
 "HUMAN IS….CORRECT! MOVE ONTO THE NEXT
SPHINX!" boomed Sphinx Two, looking slightly disappointed that
its riddle had been solved.
"You are headed for planet Destro, above the planet of Clix. To get
there, you must use the Katapolt."
"STEP FORWARD!" boomed the second Sphinx.
"This next riddle has answers two,
answer them both to get through!"
"The first ever humans didn't have something. What was it?"

"I know the first one, Maree," said Sam.
"And I think I know the second," said Nick.
"The first answer is parents," said Sam to the Sphinx.
"And the second…bellybutton." added Nick.
"How do you know that?" asked Ceirin, looking at Nick. "You
don't have a bellybutton!"

41

"Thankfully! Bellybuttons are weird." Nick replied.

"CORRECT! MOVE ONTO THE NEXT SPHINX!" boomed Sphinx Three.

"You are headed for planet Destro, above the planet of Clix. To get there, you must use the Katapolt. It can be found on an island of Clix's coast."

"STEP FORWARD!" boomed the fourth Sphinx.

"A man and woman were driving in a car. The man decided to go for help at a nearby petrol station. He made sure nobody was in the car apart from his wife, rolled all the windows up and locked the door. He went off, but when he came back, his wife lay dead, and a stranger was in the car. No physical damage was done to the car. How did the stranger get in?"

Ceirin knew this one; he had seen it a long time ago while searching the internet.

"The stranger was a baby, the woman died in childbirth."

"CORRECT! MOVE ONTO THE NEXT SPHINX!" boomed Sphinx Four.

"You are headed for planet Destro, above the planet of Clix. To get there, you must use the Katapolt. It can be found on an island of Clix's coast. The island lies to the west."

"STEP FORWARD!" boomed the fifth Sphinx.

"A time when they're green, a time when they're brown,
But both of these times, they cause me to frown,
But just in between, for a very short while,
They're perfect and yellow and cause me to smile,
What am I talking about?"

The riddles were getting harder.

"Ceirin, what do you think it is?" whispered Maree, so that the Sphinx wouldn't hear.

"All I can think of is leaves…"

"But yellow leaves don't make me smile…"

"HURRY," the Sphinx urged.

"We don't have the time to think of anything else!" said Sam.

"It's all we've got…" sighed Nick.

"The answer is….Leaves!" said Maree.

"THE ANSWER IS…INCORRECT! NOW YOU MUST FIGHT!" instantly, the Sphinx threw herself at Sam, knocking her flying.

"Nick! block her next attack!" shouted Ceirin. Nick transformed himself into a huge white sheet, and threw himself over the Sphinx.

"Sam! Quickly! Help Nick!" cried Maree. The sphinx was tearing wildly at the sheet, leaving deep rips into the fabric.

"Nick! Fly away!" yelled Ceirin. Nick turned into a raven, and flew into the sky, squawking loudly. But as he rose, the Sphinx raised a paw and batted him out of the sky.

While the Sphinx was distracted, Sam rose behind her and landed onto the Sphinxes eyes, and dug in her claws. A howl came from the creature and blood spurted from her eyes.

"Yuck…" Ceirin said.

"You need to battle more often." Maree said, unfazed by the blood. Then, Sam fired a bolt of lightning at the Sphinx, setting its hair and fur alight.

"Sam, charge up!" instructed Maree. While the Sphinx tried to roll out the fire, electricity gathered between Sam's horns. "Then do a double attack!"

She fired a jet of water over as much of the Sphinx as she could, before releasing a bolt of lightning. It was conducted by the water, causing the Sphinx even more pain.

"The…answer…was bananas… the…island…is…the… second… away…from….the…shore…" said the Sphinx, and lay still, before slowly dissolving into sand.

"Is that all we need?" Ceirin asked Maree.

"No…there must be more, if there are more sphinx," replied Maree.

"STEP FORWARD!" boomed the sixth Sphinx. It seemed slightly shocked by the fifth Sphinx's defeat.

There is a word in the English language in which the first two

letters signify a male; the first three signify a female, the first four a great male, the whole word a great female. What is the word?"
Ceirin had pulled out his PDA, and had started drawing on it with a touch pen.

"Do we really have time for that?" asked Maree, making sure she kept out of earshot from the Sphinx.

"I'll be quick." said Ceirin, scribbling something. "If the first two and first three letters signify a male and female, they must be He and Her. That must make the next word Hero and the answer...Heroine!"

"HEROINE IS...CORRECT! MOVE ON TO THE NEXT SPHINX!" boomed the sixth Sphinx.

"You are headed for planet Destro, above the planet of Clix. To get there, you must use the Katapolt. It can be found on an island of Clix's coast. It is the second island from the shore. To use the Katapolt, you need a magical item."

"STEP FORWARD!" boomed the seventh Sphinx.

"A faerie and an imp take part in a 100 metre race against each other. When the faerie crossed the finish line, the imp was only at the ninety metre mark. The faerie suggested they run another race. This time, the faerie started ten metres away from the start. All other things being equal, will the imp win, lose, or will it be a tie?"

"When they race, the faerie will be ten metres faster, so they will both reach the finish line at the same time. Then, the faster of the two will win, the faerie. So the imp will lose," said Sam. She and Maree always had challenges and races underwater, and she had gotten used to working out such problems.

"LOSE IS CORRECT!" boomed the Sphinx. With all this boom-ing, everyone was getting a headache.

"You are headed for planet Destro, above the planet of Clix. To get there, you must use the Katapolt. It can be found on an island of Clix's coast. It is the second island from the shore. To use the Katapolt, you need a magical item. This item is the Phoenix Feather. "

"STEP FORWARD!" boomed the eighth Sphinx.

"If you solve my riddle in time,
I'll let you skip Sphinx number nine!" laughed the Sphinx. It
seemed younger than all the other Sphinx, and looked more like a
girl than a woman.
*"Seven people met each other, and each shook hands only once
with each of the others, how many handshakes will there have
been? Think carefully, it's not as simple as it seems!"*
"Easy!" said Maree, "Fort-"
"Wait a minute…" said Sam, hurriedly covering Maree's mouth.
"It said it wasn't as simple as it seems…"
"It must be a trick!" agreed Ceirin. "I'll draw up a diagram on my
PDA." He typed away for a few minutes. The Sphinx tapped its
paw impatiently, causing the ground to shake.
"Are computers allowed?" she asked.
"I guess so. It's a computer game!" Sam replied.
"Look!" Ceirin said, "At first glance it seems to be forty-two, but
when two people shake hands, that counts as two shakes, so-"
"Ceirin, we don't have a clue what you're on about, just get to the
answer!"
"…So it's only half that, twenty-one!"
"CORRECT! And you managed to do it in less than 5 minutes!
You get to skip Sphinx Nine!" Then she added under her breath,
"Which is good, the last tamer destroyed Sphinx Nine, and I was
going to have to take her place!"
"Are you old enough for this job?" asked Sam rudely.
"Actually, no. But with all the tamers coming and killing us, we're
short staffed. "
"Sphinxes…short of staff?" asked Nick.
"Well it is virtual *reality*, these things happen. Now, do you want
that clue or would you prefer a nice chat and a cup of tea?"
"Actually, that tea sound rather-" started Ceirin, stopping when he
saw everyone glaring at him. "Well, *I* didn't know it was a rhetori-
cal question, did I?"
"You are headed for planet Destro, above the planet of Clix. To
get there, you must use the Katapolt. It can be found on an island
of Clix's coast. It is the second island from the shore. To use the

Katapolt, you need a magical item. This item is the Phoenix Feather. To use it, you need a spell. The codeword for this spell is *LinksofChain!*" She paused to breathe, then continue. "Also, Sphinx Ten is a bit different to the other Sphinxes, No riddles; you automatically have to battle her. And don't get distracted by her looks, she's distracted many tamers that way!" said Sphinx Eight, winking at Ceirin.

"Ooooooooh!" said Sam and Maree together, "Sphinx Eight's got a crush on Ceirin!" Both Ceirin and the Sphinx blushed red. "I do not!" they exclaimed in unison.

"By the way, since you're one of the first living players I have seen here, you must be pretty special! If you ever need help, give me a shout!"

"How do you know we're not normal players?" Ceirin asked.

"Well, duh. The game's offline, normal player's can't play."

"Wait a minute...one of the first?" asked Maree.

"Why, yes, not too long ago, another girl was brought past here. She had been captured by one of the Destroyers servants; they had her on a chain and were treating her like a slave or something. It was kind of sad. Poor thing hadn't been fed in ages!"

"Ages? How long's it been? I can't remember when I last slept!" yawned Maree.

"Since we were transported? Three days..." said Ceirin, checking his PDA clock.

"Three days...my parents must be worried..." said Maree. She'd almost forgotten about home...and her name, as well.

"Yes...my mum will be going frantic..." said Ceirin.

"Do you think we should rest a bit before the fight?" asked Nick. He had been quiet for a while, saving up his energy. The fight had been hard for both of them, and now they would have to face an even harder Sphinx!

"Are there any save shrines nearby?" asked Sam.

"Shrines? You don't need any of those, you just go to sleep! Since you'll be needing warmth and shelter, I'd suggest going to the near-by temple." The Sphinx suggested, listening to the conversation.

"There are a lot of temples," observed Ceirin.

46

"But only one with a doorway," said the Sphinx pointedly, annoyed at their pestering.

"Come on, let's go," Nick said, heading towards it. Ceirin hesitated, but followed everyone else. What choice did they have?

Chapter 7: *Pyramid Panic*

Maree? Maree? Can you hear me?
Yes.
Have you found a way to help me yet?
No.
Say more than that!
Why should I?
Something's wrong, isn't it?
What makes you think that?
Is everyone OK? What's happened?
How could you Ellen?
How could I wh-

When Maree woke, it was still dark. She lay there, for a few minutes, in the darkness of the corner. When they arrived here, they had found that the pyramid was completely hollow, with a shrine in the centre. They had pulled some blankets and a pillow (that and other things were given to members at the beginning of the game in a starter pack).

She thought about what Ellen had said. Could she really be the snake? If she was, why was she being treated to badly? Maybe she was innocent...and Maree had just been really mean to her.

Her thoughts were interrupted by voices from outside.

"How dare you interfere with the game!? You shouldn't try to help them! They tried to destroy us!"

"They are special. They have a task to complete. We must aid them!" That voice was familiar. Sphinx Eight? What was she doing now!

"You are a traitor to us all, Sphinx Eight! Stand aside or perish!"

"You cannot interfere with the game! You said so yourself!"

"This is different! We cannot disobey his orders! He said we must destroy them!"

"He! *He*? What about *them*!"

"STAND ASIDE!"

"NO!" There was a pause, as though the Sphinxes had heard something. Maree froze. Suddenly, Sphinx Eight started talking again.

"You are headed for planet Destro, above the planet of Clix. To get there, you must use the Katapolt. It can be found on an island of Clix's coast. It is the second island from the shore. To use the Katapolt, you need a magical item. This item is the Phoenix Feather. To use it, you need a spell. The codeword for this spell is *LinksofChain*! The Phoenix feather can be found in a chest that Sphinx Ten guards. At the back of the pyramid, there is a secret exit. Find it!"

As she said this, there was a crash as something, most likely Sphinx Eight, was slammed the pyramid.

She ran through to wake the others. Ceirin was fast asleep, Nick beside him in the form of a Teddy Bear, snoring slightly.

"Ceirin, Nick, Sam, wake up, we have to go!"

"What?" said Ceirin sleepily, yawning. "Where's the fire?"

"It's worse than a fire, Ceirin!" cried Maree. They had to hurry!

"Earthquake!" Nick yelled, standing up and tripping over his bear-paws. He looked at himself. "Um...you didn't see that!"

"What is it?" asked Sam, wide awake.

"The Sphinx are trying to kill us! We have to get out!"

"But how?" squeaked Nick, forgetting he was still a bear.

"There's a back door! Follow me!" shouted Maree, gathering up all her belongings and storing them in her rucksack.

"Come on, hurry up!" cried Nick, changing into a hare and thump-ing his back legs impatiently. Looking back, Maree saw the walls of the pyramid crumble behind him, and a giant lion's paw come crashing through.

"As soon as we get out, we have to grab the feather inside Sphinx Ten's chest, before it can stop us! Three...two...one..." Maree pressed a slightly different looking brick in the pyramid's walls, and the wall seemed to reassemble itself to form a door in its middle.

49

"Wow…" said Ceirin, "Cool Special Effects!"

They charged through the door, veering round the corners and back too the riddle grounds. They could hear the thumping of the sphinx paws as they pounded across the sand towards them. In front of them, a cliff edge was coming closer…and closer…

Nick, in eagle form, was the first to spot the chest, half buried beneath the sand. He called out, and everyone ran towards him. Maree was the first human to reach it, and, after wasting precious seconds fumbling with the catch, she managed to open the chest. Inside it lay a feather, dappled with oranges, yellows and reds to make it look like it was on fire. And, as Maree held it, she found it was hot, but not hot enough to burn her. Sphinx Ten had almost reached them. They could feel the heat from his fire as he shot flame after flame at them.

Everyone took hold of the feather, and Maree said the spell word Sphinx Eight had told her.

"I must cast this spell, now or never,
LinksofChain I say to the Phoenix Feather!"

Maree suddenly doubled over as a shooting pain shot down her back. Had Sphinx Ten reached them? Looking over, she saw her comrades doing the same, but there was no fire.

And as quickly as it came, the pain left. Looking round, Maree saw that wings had appeared on each human, fiery coloured like the Phoenix feather. Above them, a Phoenix flew in circles.

"Heed you now the Phoenix's call,
Fly away, fly away, fly away all!" it cried, before disappearing in a flash of flame.

Everyone immediately obeyed its command, and it was just as well, for as soon as they were in the air a burst of flame scorched the sand where they had stood.

Sphinx Ten roared angrily as they disappeared into the sandstorm. He turned towards Sphinx Eight, but she too had vanished.

Chapter 8: *The Mini Game Festival*

"So, where did Sphinx Eight say we should go again?" asked Ceirin.

"It can be found on an island of Clix's coast. It is the second island from the shore," called a voice from behind him. Shocked, Ceirin looked behind him, and saw Sphinx Eight, flapping hard on huge wings.

"I thought you might need a hand flying through the storm!" she shouted, and flew closer. As she did so, her wings blew away all the incoming sand, making it a lot easier for them to fly.

"And if you'd stayed you'd be in trouble with the others." Sam added.

"Exactly," the Sphinx agreed.

"Thanks for your help!" Maree said. "That was brave, going against the others!"

Sam laughed at the huge creature struggling to control its wings. "So what's so important about these wings, anyway? Couldn't Maree and Ceirin just ride on us?" asked Sam, giggling.

"I can't tell you that, but they're important." Sphinx Eight replied mysteriously.

"I wonder if the Creator knows about the destroyer..." said Maree after a while.

"I'd think so. Isn't the Destroyer something he programmed into the game?" asked Nick.

"Of course he is, he makes up everything to do with the game!" said Ceirin.

After that, they flew in silence, trying to see anything through the sand.

"Are we there yet?" asked Nick in cockatiel form, yawning with boredom.

"Actually, yes," said Maree, landing on Katapolt Island. Sphinx Eight turned round.

51

"I cannot come with you any further." She said sadly. "Good luck on your quest, I hope you find that girl you were looking for!" she called, flying off.

"Wait!" called Maree after her, "What about these wings?"

"They will disappear once you land, simply repeat the spell and they will return! If you use them often enough, you may not even need the spell or the feather!" she called faintly, disappearing into the foggy sky.

As they landed, they noticed the island wasn't anywhere near as small as they'd thought.

"What's that?" asked Ceirin, pointing to a metal construction in the middle of the island.

"It looks like a…fairground…" said Nick

Maree shivered. And it wasn't from the cold. Deserted fairgrounds always meant trouble.

Nick wrapped himself around her neck in cat form, in an attempt to warm her. She shook him off, telling him it was all right.

"You look good as a cat, Nick." Ceirin said, looking at him.

"I'm not a big fan of cats…" Nick replied, changing into a Yorkshire terrier.

"We shouldn't go…" Maree said doubtfully. "We should try and find the Katapolt."

"I don't see it anywhere. The fairground must have something to do with it," said Sam. She tried to fly behind the fairground, and banged into an invisible wall

"There's a force field to stop us leaving. We have to go in," she said.

"Great. Just fantastic…" groaned Maree. "A deserted fairground."

"Maree…" said Ceirin, peering through the gate, "I don't think this fairground is deserted…"

Everyone peered round and saw, instead of creaking Ferris Wheels and damaged wooden stalls, a bright funfair packed with sound and lights, and filled with players.

"What is this?" Sam asked a stall owner when they entered.

"Why this is the Dragon Realm Mini Game Festival!" he said with a grin.

"How long has this been here?" Maree asked a passing player.

"Since one o'clock this morning, so that players in different time zones could enjoy it!"

"What time is it?" Sam asked. Katapolt Island had been too foggy to see whether it was day or night.

"Half past eleven at night." said Ceirin, looking at his PDA clock.

"Come on, let's go on some rides!" cried Sam and Maree together, running off towards the rollercoaster.

"Do we think we should follow her?" asked Nick doubtfully.

"What could happen?" replied Ceirin.

"Famous last words…" muttered Nick darkly.

But they both followed Maree, checking out the rides and stalls. Within ten minutes, they all had armfuls of food and prizes. Ceirin had excelled at all the games, beating everyone's high score. But Maree ended up with most of the prizes, like the soft toys and posters.

"Come on, let's go on the rollercoaster!" shouted Maree over the noise of the crowd, cramming her prizes in her bag.

When she got there, she found that there was a long line of people waiting to go on.

"Don't worry about the queues!" called a clown from the roller-coaster entrance.

"If you wait for the midnight ride, you'll get on a special, extra large rollercoaster that can hold EVERYONE!" Upon hearing this, the crowd cheered, and everyone at the other rides also joined the queue.

"Are you coming on?" Maree called to Ceirin, standing amongst the crowd.

"No thanks, I can't stand crowds," he said, walking off to a corner and switching on his PDA. It wasn't just the crowd that spooked him. Something seemed odd about this 'Midnight Ride'.

"What's wrong, Ceirin?" asked Nick, lying beside him in the form of a black Labrador.

"I don't understand what the fairground is doing here…" he said, frowning.

"We followed the Sphinx's instructions exactly…so where's the Katapolt?"

"That's a good question," said Nick." Unfortunately, I can't answer it."

"Well, that sure is helpful!" exclaimed Ceirin, stroking Nick.

"Last call for the Midnight Ride!" shouted the clown. "Room for everyone!" More people joined the line. The rest of the stalls and games were deserted now, Ceirin was the only one not on the ride. It was a huge roller coaster, starting with a steep drop of more than two hundred metres, into the mouth of a huge metal crocodile. They had started to board the ride now. By a minute to twelve, everyone was on and the ride was ready to start.

As the clock in the centre of the fairground started to chime, the ride started. With each chime, a different thought entered Ceirin's mind.

One…The ride was starting to move.

Two…The Rails all snapped down, securing the riders.

Three…People were walking towards the ride.

Four…It was the stall owners.

Five…They don't look too well…

Six…Wait! Did that Crocodile just move?

Seven…It's moving! The Crocodile's moving!

Eight…Those snapping jaws look pretty dangerous…

Nine…Why are people screaming?

Ten…Must be scarier than it looks…

Eleven…I wonder if it's dangerous…

Twelve…Wait a minute…What in the Realm's happening?

The crocodile had sprung to life, and was eagerly stomping along the rails towards the rollercoaster, it's eyes shining.

"Ceirin! Wake up! The riders are in danger!" shouted Nick suddenly. He transformed into a huge Golden Eagle, and Ceirin quickly hopped on.

"Nick, fly up to the ride and I'll see if I can get Maree out." Ceirin said, oblivious of the panic around him. As long as Nick was with him, nothing could go wrong.

Nick flew up, rising steadily. Soon they would be up there, and they could get the members out. Was this what the Creator called a challenge? Within minutes, they had reached Maree.

"Nick! Ceirin! Help!" she called. The safety railings had clamped down tightly, trapping them. Sam was ignoring Ceirin, staring at something behind him.

Ceirin turned. Behind him, the fair was disappearing! As it disappeared, the stall owners massed even tightly together, waiting for something to happen.

One of them noticed Nick, and brought out a gun, aiming at the Eagle. But before he could fire, moonlight filled the area, and Ceirin was temporarily blinded.

While he hid his eyes, there were cries from the stall owners, and when the light faded again in their place stood a mass of wolves, growling wildly.

Except for one owner, still in human form, struggling to stop the transformation. It was the one with the gun, and before anyone realised it he had fired a black sphere a Nick, and transformed into a wolf just as the shot left the gun.

The Eagle cried in pain as the sphere hit him. Then he froze, and started falling quickly to the ground.

"Nick!" cried Ceirin, clinging to his falling dragon.

"Get off, free the others!" he grunted.

"How?" replied Ceirin. The ground was getting pretty close. No answer from Nick, his mouth had also been frozen. He looked round and saw some of the rollercoaster riders had gotten out and were trying to climb down the frame that held the rails up. He would have to join them.

He jumped off Nick, and for a brief moment floated, the force of his jump and gravity pulling him down both cancelling each other out. Then he reached out to grab a railing, and everything returned to normal, with him hanging for dear life from a rickety pole.

He was tempted to cast the Phoenix Feather spell, but if he did so he might knock another player off. He was going to have to climb. For one of the first times during the game, Ceirin was scared. Nick was tangled up somewhere in the poles below, and he was all alone, above a pack of snarling wolves and below a giant metal, living crocodile. Not an ideal spot to hang out.

Summoning together all his courage, he started to climb. The poles were slippery from the fog, and many snapped as he stood on them.

The fairground was still disappearing. If he didn't hurry, it would soon reach the rollercoaster. However, the gates were not being deleted. That must be the only way out of this area.

He finally reached the top, but the rails were too thin to stand beside the rollercoaster. Precious minutes ticked away as Ceirin tried to lift up the bar without falling.

"It's no use!" he said, beads of sweat dripping down his face, "I have to get the computer to lift the bars up!"

He sidled along until he reached the front of the rollercoaster, and was about to step onto the rails when he heard a yell. In front of him, another player had stepped onto the rails, but had put both feet of each of the rail sides and been electrocuted, disappearing from the game immediately, along with his Dragon, a brown pterodactyl.

Carefully, Ceirin stepped between the rails, and wrenched open the front of the rollercoaster.

Inside was a mass of wire, in a range of different colours. He wouldn't have time to fiddle with them all.

Without thinking about what might happen, he brought out a knife, and split open all the wire.

As soon as he did this, he felt a shooting pain course through his body, along with thousands of volts of electricity.

The rollercoaster went haywire, the rails going up and down and the lights flashing on and off. As soon as people realised what was happening, they jumped out and started trying to get down.

Maree jumped on Sam and flew round to where Ceirin had been thrown by the blast. He had smashed into a cardboard figure, designed to come out of the tunnel the Crocodile had once guarded. He was completely black, and lay still, flames crackling across his hair and clothes. Maree tipped a healing potion down his open mouth, but he didn't wake. Sam covered him with a blast of icy water, and he got up with a start.

Remembering what was happening, he asked where Nick was. Sam scanned the fairground, and eventually saw him, in mouse form, hiding in a corner of a stall as the werewolf owner sniffed the ground, searching for him.

Before they could call down, they felt the rails start to sway from side to side.

"What's happening?" asked Maree, struggling to keep her balance. "The frame's being deleted, we have to get off!" he replied. Sam flew up into the air, and Maree and Ceirin both cast the Phoenix Feather spell and followed her.

Nick spotted them, and called for them to get the wolves away. Sam fired a jet of water at them, and while they shook themselves dry Nick flew away in falcon form.

It was when he did this that the full damage his fall had caused could be seen. He flew awkwardly, one wing bent at an odd angle, his eyes dull and his feathers ruffled. He changed size, becoming larger, and picked up Ceirin.

They flew low, trying to get out of the gates. The wolves saw this, returning to their human forms and running to the gates. They only just swooped through in time.

Five seconds after they had escaped, the doors closed with a bang behind them.

They landed on the sandy beach of the island, looking at the chaos around them.

There were wails as friends, dragons and humans alike were trapped behind the gates, and moans of annoyance after coming to the island and not finding the Katapolt.

As the minutes ticked away, the door started to fall apart, deleted bit by bit. Humans and dragons disappeared as their counterparts were deleted on the other side.

Gradually, all the remaining humans started to leave.

"Should we go?" asked Sam.

"No." said Ceirin firmly. "We have to rest, we need time to heal." They settled down on the sand, twisting and turning as it scratched at their skin of scales, until eventually they all fell fast asleep.

Chapter 9: *The Katapolt*

"Hurry up, keep moving!"

"Can't we stop? Just for a minute!"

"No! We have to get all these players inside!"

"But we've had almost no rest! First you take us to a pyramid, then you move us in those flying cages to this tower, and now you're bringing in all these players! And in between, we're only allowed about an hour to sleep!"

"Keep moving, or that horse's going to the Knackers Yard!"

"Leave Crystal alone! Ow!" Ellen yelped, as the robot's leather whip struck her across the face.

"That'll teach you..." murmured the android, walking off.

"Ellen..." sighed Crystal.

"How are we meant to escape if we don't have the strength, Crystal?"

"I have plenty of strength." Crystal said angrily. "I'm stronger than ever!"

"Those pills they give you, the ones that put your stats up so quickly, they're against game rules!"

"Without them, I'd probably have died by now!"

"They're probably killing you!"

"It won't be for much longer! I'll get us out of here, I promise!"

"I know you will, Crystal." Ellen said, stroking the horse's mane.

"Shush, something's happening." Crystal said.

She had been kept there for a long time. They robots would hit her with stones or whip her if she didn't do what she was told.

"Hurry!" said a robot. "If we keep them here much longer, they'll be evacuated from the game!"

"They're getting too hungry in the real world. I remember reading that if you do, you'll be evacuated from the game." Ellen said.

She had read the whole rulebook while trapped in one of the

cages with nothing to do.

"I hear Ellen has been causing trouble," a voice said. All the robots sprang to attention.

"It's sorted now, master," said one.

"So it's true! There was trouble. Send the pair through!"

Ellen and Crystal were jostled roughly into the room.

"Welcome," said the voice. Ellen looked round.

"You cannot see me," the voice said. "But I am here. You have been acting against my will, causing trouble. I will not abide that kind of behavior."

A silver haired girl entered the room, along with a white snake-like dragon with no legs or arms, that hovered in mid air.

"What is this? I didn't read about it on fan sites…" she muttered. "Is it a Mini Game?"

"Of a sort," said the Voice. "A test. Do not be afraid. Stay still and calm, and you shall be released with many rewards. Do not mind the girl, she is merely here to watch."

"Rewards?" the girl said. "Great!" She stood still, waiting. Suddenly, there was a loud bang, and she fell lifeless to the floor.

"Yes," the voice replied. "Rewarded with a quick death."

Ellen gasped, and Crystal whinnied in fright.

"Don't worry. It's not your time yet. When it is, it'll be much, much worse. You have been warned. Do not give me another reason to notice you."

*　　　*　　　*

When Maree, Sam, Ceirin and Nick awoke that morning, they found the Gateway gone, and in its place the black and grey Katapolt.

"Is this the thing that's meant to take us to Destro?" asked Nick, eying the contraption suspiciously.

"Yes. It's the only way," said Ceirin.

"At least now we know we're at the right place. It's cleverly hidden." said Sam.

"It must be awfully high up, if you need to use this thing."

"Are you sure the weather is right for this?" asked Maree, staring up at a grey sky.

"I don't think it'll get much better..." said Ceirin. "We might as well go now."

"Nick, transform into something with wings, Maree, let's cast the Phoenix Feather spell," said Ceirin. Nick transformed into an Albatross again, and Maree and Ceirin both cast the spell.

"Let's test it. Nick, step onto the Katapolt," said Ceirin.

"Why do I have to be a guinea pig?"

"Because you're smart and clever and a quick shape-shifter."

"Was that flattery or sarcasm?"

"You decide. Now step on the Katapolt."

Nick stepped carefully onto the Katapolt. Above him flashed a message:

Wings: Yes. Access to Destro: Granted.

Nick stepped off. Ceirin picked up a stone and placed it on the Katapolt.

Wings: No. Access to Destro: Denied.

Then the Katapolt whirred into life, and hurled the stone to the ground with such force it shattered into hundreds of small pieces. Then Ceirin whispered something into Nick's ear, and placed another rock on his back.

Error: Each Passenger must have Wings!

The Katapolt whirred into life once more, and Nick hurriedly flew off. The rock, however, was pulled back onto the Katapolt by an invisible force, and was also hurled to the ground.

"Wow," said Maree, "That thing is smart!".

Nervously, everyone piled onto the Katapolt.

Wings: Yes. Access to Destro: Granted

Appeared over everyone's head. They waited, and another message appeared.

Katapolt Launching...

It whirred into life once more, and launched them all into the air. They scattered, flying up at an astounding speed. Before they knew it, they were flying towards a giant floating mass of land. Everyone quickly spread their wings to stop their flight, and landing in a heap on the ground. Now Maree knew why she had to get her own wings, she would have been flung off Sam's back and smashed into the ground if she'd ridden on her.

Destro hung suspended in mid air, above masses of land and sea. Above, the sun bathed the land in a golden light as it set. It was so beautiful...surely no game could be like this?

Above them floated a large tower, suspended in thin air.

"What *is* that?" asked Nick.

"It's a floating tower, what did you think it looked like?" said Sam sarcastically.

"I'm going under it quickly," said Maree, dashing over to the other side.

"Come on Maree, nothing's going to happen!" Ceirin said, following her.

"See, nothing!" he said when he passed under it. Just as he said this, a girl fell on his head.

Chapter 10: *The Guardian*

"Ellen!" cried Maree in shock. "Where'd you come from?"

"Up there," she said, pointing up to a window.

"So, met anyone new?" she asked, looking round.

"Yes, a boy called Ceirin. Where did he go?" Maree said. Nick laughed.

From underneath Ellen's pile of sheets came Ceirin's muffled voice.

"Oh dear…" said Ellen, lifting the sheets and blushing as Ceirin climbed out. He was red faced and his hair was a mess.

"You!" he said, glaring at her.

"Yes me, why?" asked Ellen. A sharp shake of head from Maree told Ceirin he shouldn't mention their suspicions.

"You're the one we've been looking for!" exclaimed Ceirin.

"Where were you? asked Maree as Crystal hovered down from the tower.

"Ellen! I told you to *hold on* to me when I was flying," she said.

"Oh, hello everyone, good to see you. We should run, before they let out the falcons," Crystal said distractedly.

"The what!?" shouted Sam and Maree in unison.

"They're going to let out some falcons to keep track of our movement, and then they'll start opening trap doors underneath our feet until they've caught all of us." explained Ellen. "We need to hide before they spot us."

"Where exactly are we meant to hide?" asked Maree.

"Oh dear…I didn't realise this area was so open…"

"Why didn't you escape earlier…?" groaned Ceirin.

"Well, at first I thought it was part of the plot. Then I got bored and finally read the rulebook. I was looking at the plot section and realised it wasn't part of it, so decided to escape. And, due to some strange coincidence, you happened to be passing by at the time," explained Ellen.

"So now you're not a newbie, but a n00b," sighed Sam.

"What's the difference?" asked Ellen. Behind her, Crystal laughed. A bird called from the floating prison tower, and everyone started running.

"I still don't get it!" shouted Ellen as Crystal pushed her after them.

"Hey, Nick, why are you wolf-formed? Why not go as an Emu for a change?" shouted Sam, running with Nick at the front of the group.

"What in the realm's an Emu?"

"It's this cool bird, like an Ostrich. It beats a wolf by far!"

"No way, wolves are the best!" replied Nick.

"Emus are!"

"Wolves!"

"Both of you! Stop arguing and keep running!" yelled Crystal.

"It's no use! Those birds are designed for speed," shouted Ellen.

"Like an Emu." Ceirin said, nodding.

"We'll have to stand and fight!" Ellen continued, ignoring him. The falcons had been released, and they were quickly catching up with the group. Behind them flew a group of Kilimario, holding the controls for dropping the cages.

"We'll need to take down the Kilimario first, so they don't drop the cages while we're fighting," said Nick.

"It's us they're after. We'll try and lead the birds away." Ellen said, jumping onto Crystal.

"I'll fight with my sword." added Maree.

Suddenly, the cages started to fall. Huge glass boxes fell from the sky, most aimed at Ellen.

"Good luck everyone!" shouted Ellen as they galloped away. The Falcons split into two groups, one after Ellen and the other staying with the rest of the dragons. The Kilimario also split into two, one group staying in the air to drop cages, the others landing to fight.

"These ones look strange," Said Nick. They seemed tougher than normal Kilimario, designed for battle instead of sending messages, with tougher skin, sharper claws, and a bag full of weapons instead of messages.

"Kilimario aren't meant to fight. How did they change?" asked Sam.

"Who knows what they've done to them up in Destro?" Maree drew her sword, glowing brightly, and ran towards them. Sam and Nick ran after her, and the attack started.

Avoiding having to fight without a weapon, Ceirin ran past the fight, behind the Kilimario, and grabbed one from behind. He clamped his hand round its mouth and dragged it to the ground. As it tried to get up, he kicked it in the head, knocking it unconscious. Leaving it there for the others to destroy, he went for another.

"Sam, where's Ceirin?" Nick called up to Sam as he pounded Dragons in Gorilla-form.

"He's at the back of the Kilimario, attacking them from behind," Sam shouted from the air, trying to attack some of the birds that kept lunging at her. The Air Kilimario were nearby, but they weren't dropping any cages in case they hit one of their fighters.

In the thick of the fight, Ceirin was swinging at the Kilimario with a sword he had stolen from an unconscious Kilimario. While he was swinging, one of the fighters struck and bit his arm. He yelled as its sharp teeth plunged into his skin, and kicked it off, finishing it with his sword. But it was his sword hand that had been bitten, and he was in too much pain to fight with it.

Swinging awkwardly with his other hand, he managed to escape the fighters and had a chance to look at the wound. It was deep, and such a mess that he couldn't look at it without feeling sick. He had a healing potion, but it would take too long to work. As he tried to think what to do his mind started to cloud, and his vision became slightly faded at the edges. He was blacking out. A cage landed to his right, and he realised as well that he was now a target for the cages.

Far away from the group, Ellen and Crystal were trying to escape the birds. They're every move was tracked, and the cage throws were becoming more accurate. Soon they would either be trapped or crushed by one of the glass cubes.

"What are we going to do?" shouted Ellen over the eager cries of the falcons.

"Fly up and attack!" replied Crystal, spreading her wings. Ellen hurriedly adjusted her grip so the wings wouldn't knock her off Crystal.

The horse dragon rose into the air, and swung round, knocking away the falcons by turning quickly and hitting them with her wings. A cage suddenly appeared in the air over them, and they had to swerve to the side as it dropped down, bringing with it a lot of the birds.

The remaining still attacked, but Ellen realised they were avoiding her.

"Crystal, why are they avoiding me?"

"You haven't got a weapon, and haven't tried to attack them, so you're protected by the game rules. But they can still try to capture you, or harm you in a way that doesn't involve them fighting you."

"What do you mean?"

"They're trying to bring me down, so that you'll fall with me," explained Crystal, slowing down. "Why are they bringing more falcons over there?"

"One of the others might need help. We have to go see!"

"Hang on, this might get rough!" warned Crystal, turning around sharply and flying towards the others.

From near Ceirin, one of the unconscious Dragons was stirring. It was staring at him groggily as it came round. Before Ceirin could get away, it had realised who he was.

"Drop the cages! One of them is injured, and out in the open!" it shouted.

Some of the Kilimario fighters started coming towards him.

"What are they doing? Are they retreating?" asked Maree, in the middle of the fighters.

"No, something has happened. We have to go see!" said Nick, evidently worrying about Ceirin. They charged through the crowd, until they saw Ceirin lying surrounded by the fighters, blood all over him.

"How are we going to get past those things before he passes out, or is caged?" asked Nick, shape-shifting into a kangaroo and kicking away a fighter.

"An aerial attack," suggested Sam, landing next to them. She shot a blast of electricity at the enemies, shocking quite a few.

"Whatever we do, we should hurry" added Maree.

"Look! Crystal and Ellen are here! Maybe they can distract the group while we charge them."

"I'll go tell them," said Nick, shape-shifting again into an Emu and flapping his wings. "Hey, why won't these things work?"

"Nick, Emus can't fly!"

"Then why are they birds?!" shouted Nick, changing yet again into his favoured Golden Eagle form. He flew up to Crystal, nearly colliding with her because she was flying so fast. They hovered for a moment, and then rushed at the Dragons at full speed. They scattered, and Maree and Sam charged, bowling over the remaining guards.

"Oh, hello guys. Meet my new friends, Jimmy-Bob, Bobby-John, Big Bobby, Bobby Junior..." cried Ceirin happily as they picked him up.

"Is he going to be alright?" asked Nick as he dragged Ceirin onto his back.

"Guess what! I can pull my hand off!" Ceirin yelled.

"I hope so..." murmured Maree.

"Look! I'm on a kitty!" He shouted at a rock.

"This is just embarrassing..." moaned Nick. Sam swooped down to pick up Maree, and Nick changed into a flying couch and followed them.

Below, the few Kilimario that remained growled, but didn't follow.

"I'm a flying piggy!" yelled Ceirin, trying to stand up but failing.

"Ellen. Can you get onto the couch and give Ceirin a healing potion? It will take a while to heal his hand, but it should help calm him down and stop him trying to jump down and see Jimmy-Bob." asked Nick, rolling his eyes.

"Nancy! You came to give me my shortbread!" Ceirin told Nick, before fainting.

"Well, at least he's stopped yelling..." remarked Ellen as she tried to stand on the couch without overbalancing.

"This is my bathroom..." muttered Ceirin in his sleep.

"I hope you're not serious!" exclaimed Nick.

Ellen took off his bag and put him in the recovery position, then took out the healing potion he got in his starter pack. Then she pored half of it down his throat, to try and cure any internal bleeding, and poured the rest over his hand. They continued on until they finally reached the entrance to Destro, a large garden with a path in the middle leading to a large ornamental gateway.

"Wow...posh. Can we rest here? I think everyone's tired from that battle." said Sam. Everyone agreed, except Ceirin, who was too busy murmuring about how Emus would take over the world.

They settled down, grateful to have the soft grass to lie on. It was a warm night, probably because Destro shared the climate of Clix, right below it.

"You know, Sam, it's strange how a place containing such evil can be so pleasant," whispered Maree as she was falling asleep.

"Maybe it wasn't always evil..." yawned Sam.

"And maybe...Ellen isn't the Snake," decided Maree under her breath. It wasn't really maybe, she was sure about it. All Ellen's acts today had convinced her that she was as sincere as she seemed.

That night, Maree slept silently and deeply, untroubled by any more attempts to contact her through her dreams.

*   *   *

That morning, Ceirin had fully recovered, except for some scars. They woke up and started gathering their stuff together, though no one was sure whether they'd be able to use it again. This was it, the final level, the end of the game.

This was what everything had led up to; this was what they were sent to do. But would they be able to complete the game?

They had to. The entire realm was counting on them.

And so, with doubts filling their mind but with a fierce determination, they walked towards the gateway and towards the unbeatable level. At least, unbeatable if you were a normal player.

As soon as they approached the gates, they swung open with a loud creak, and the creature that guarded it stirred in its sleep. It was a huge snake; its body forking into two tails, each around three metres long, its body six metres, and its hooded face more than ten metres wide. The thick body was a dark, slimy green, dappled with black. Its fangs were long and needle sharp, dripping venom and each taller than two metres.

Everyone froze as it turned towards them, eyes open. Then it gave a moan, and closed its eyes again with a small snore. With a sigh of relief, the group moved forward. Crystal rose into the air, with Sam and hummingbird Nick following.

Instantly, the snake struck. He used one tail to hit the dragons, a blow so accurate it even hit the tiny Nick, and the other he wrapped round the humans. Then he grabbed the fallen dragons, including Nick who had turned into a rabbit in fright, and raised both tails so that both dragons and tamers were in striking range, squeezing them. "Tamersssssssssss! Dragon Tamersssssss!" It hissed, angrily. "Thinking a great creature like me would sssssssssleep while you passssssed! For thissss, you ssssssshall be punisssssssssssssssshed! What are your namessssss?" hissed the Snake, his forked tongue appearing each time he hissed. Gasping for breath, the group told him.

"You! The sssssssummoned onesssssssss! Your punisssssssshment issssssss a ssssssspecial one!" hissed the monster with glee. "You are desssssssstined for sssssssomthing worsssssssse than even I could ssssssssupply! I am glad to dissssposssssse of you, for sssssssssssoooon you ssssssshall wisssssssh I had killed you!" He hissed, his eyes glowing an eerie blue. Before they knew it, the group found themselves in a completely different area.

(hapter 11: *Fear Fork*

"Where are we? Are we still on Destro?" asked Ellen, dazed from the fall.

"No, we're not. We're in some kind of forest clearing." Sam said, looking round.

"All that and we didn't even get past the gate..." sighed Crystal.

"Fear Fork," said Crystal, reading a sign staked into the ground.

"Fear Fork? There's no fork in the path!" said Sam.

"Yeah. I wonder what th-" said Nick, before the ground started trembling.

Suddenly, the ground split into three sections, with Maree and Sam in the middle, Ceirin and Nick to the left and Ellen and Crystal to the right.

They each tried to move, but their feet were stuck fast, as the path whizzed forward at an amazing speed, twisting and turning so often everyone completely forgot where they were.

When Maree and Sam finally felt the path stop moving, they had arrived in yet another different, empty clearing.

As soon as they stepped off the path, it disappeared. Maree walked into the middle of the clearing.

"This place is completely empty," she said, walking back to where Sam stood. But she found her way blocked by a screen of glass, which turned into solid wood as she stood there.

"Sam! What's happening!" she called.

"I'm not sure. The walls seem to be closing in around you!" she called from outside, her voice muffled.

Maree felt her breath catch in her throat. She was claustrophobic.

"Sam," she called as something slid out of the walls, "There are metal spikes coming out of the walls!"

"I can't come near you, Maree! You have to get out yourself!"

"But the only people I've seen escape things like this are video game characters!" she replied.

"You are a video game character!" called Sam. She was right, thought Maree. This was a video game. She could do anything she wanted to. And in a video game, you didn't have to be claustrophobic.

As the spikes came closer, she gathered together all her courage and leapt onto the spikes, using them like steps as she climbed towards the top. The roof and the walls hadn't met yet, and there was still a gap...

She launched herself up and through the gap, but got caught half way through. She squirmed and turned around, trying to stop the roof from crushing her. Just in time, she felt a scaly claw grab at her and Sam pulled her out.

As she lay panting on the ground, there was a loud bang as each part of the box came crashing together, and then disappeared completely.

"Wow..." sighed Maree, "I'm glad that's over!" But how come, now she was out of the box, she still felt pain? Looking down, she saw her plan hadn't worked out quite as well as she thought it would. Her leg was scratched and gouged with marks from the spikes, and a ruby red river of blood flowed across the ground. She cried out at the sight of it, and tried to turn it so she couldn't see the blood, but found she couldn't. Her whole leg was red and swollen, and too painful to move. She may be a video game character, but she could still feel pain...

Sam handed her a potion, which she poured over her leg. It stung and burned, but after a minute the wound had disappeared completely.

"The swelling will go down very soon. You should be able to move now, without any pain," Sam said. "Luckily, it wasn't a deep wound. The potion could work quickly."

"Thanks, Sam," she said, pulling the leg of her trousers over it. "Let's go find the others now.

Now that the box had gone, another path could be seen in its place. Sam and Maree stepped on it, and it zoomed away once more, stopping in front of a large river.

Ceirin was standing by the edge of the riverbank, frozen with fear. Nick stood watching him, in dog form, and turned when Maree came.

"Maree! Finally! Someone able to tell me what exactly is going on here! Ceirin's frozen!"

"He must have a fear of water. You won't be allowed near him until he conquers that fear, than everything will return to normal and we can go help Ellen," explained Sam.

"So all he has to do is get over his fear and he gets out?" asked Nick.

"No" replied Maree, "It's never that simple." And as she said this, a horse appeared beside Ceirin.

"Climb on my back." It said its voice soft and soothing, "I can take you away from this place."

"Really?"

"Yes. I was sent by the Dragon Council to help you. You've been through so much, it isn't fair she should have to go to the trouble of facing your fear..."

"Thanks..." Ceirin sighed, climbed on. Anything to get away.

"Wait a minute..." said Sam, "There are no normal horses in this game!"

"That means it must be..." said Nick.

"A kelpie!" snickered the horse, its voice becoming rough and cruel, its flowing mane changing into tendrils of seaweed and its silver hair turning to a dark green.

"Ceirin! Get off!" shouted Maree.

"I can't!" cried Ceirin and they saw that, no matter how much he struggled, he was stuck fast.

The Kelpie charged towards the water, and Ceirin didn't even have time to call out before it had dived down.

"What do we do?" asked Nick, panicking.

"We wait," said Sam calmly. "It's all we can do."

"How can you be so calm?" Nick asked, staring at her.

"I'm a water dragon. I know that there's nothing to be afraid of."

What's happening? Thought Ceirin, as the Kelpie dived through the water.

*Is this what I was afraid of? It's so dark and peaceful...I think I
like it. I'm not in any pain...What is there to be afraid of? It's just
rain, that's all. What was I afraid of?*

And as he thought this, he found himself lying on the ground
where the loch had been, a path beside him. Maree was cheering.

"You did it! You conquered your fear!" she said.

"Well done!" said Sam.

"I knew you could do it, Ceirin," said Nick, beaming happily. He
transformed into a Gorilla and heaved Ceirin up.

"Come on," he grunted, "Let's go help Ellen!"

They stepped on the path, which was twice as big as the last. It
whizzed off once more, towards the edge of a forest.

When they arrived, they saw that between two trees at the front of
the forest hung a huge web.

In the middle of that web lay Ellen, wrapped tightly in a cocoon of
web. Not far away there was a giant spider, creeping slowly
towards her.

"Help, Crystal!" cried Ellen, as the giant spider came closer. In a
few minutes it would be upon her.

"Crystal, stay here! This is Ellen's fear, she has to beat it herself!"
shouted Nick.

"No!" shouted Crystal, rearing up, "Ellen has Arachnophobia! She
is terrified of spiders, I have to help her!" she said.

"You can't!" Sam said, moving to grab her back. Crystal turned
and faced Sam.

"You'd do anything to protect Maree, wouldn't you?" she asked.

"Yes." Sam said, without hesitation.

"Then I must do the same!" Crystal said, and galloped into the
web.

Instantly, her place was swapped with Ellen. She ended up in the
middle of the web, while Ellen fell to the ground, shaking with
shock.

"Crystal, look out!" she managed to cry, but it was too late. Before
the Dragon realised it, the Giant Spider had sunk its fangs into its
side.

"Ah!" screamed Crystal, whinnying in fright.

"Nick, scan Crystal's stats!" shouted Ceirin.

"She's been poisoned!" replied Nick.

"Get out of there!" cried Maree. Crystal kicked at the web, but it held fast.

"*GotProtection*!" shouted Ellen. Instantly, a round shield surrounded Crystal. The Dragon started chewing at the web, before the Spider started attacking the shield. The basic shield spell was quite weak, and could not stand up to the spiders attack.

Luckily, the Giant Spider was too busy trying to spin web round it (which merely slid off), or climb over (which was impossible due to the shields smooth surface).

But, just as Crystal chewed away the last of the web cocoon, the spider charged, destroying the shield and knocking Crystal out of the web, which disappeared along with the spider. Ellen ran over to her. She was deathly pale, the wound in her side was now red and sore.

"Crystal!" Ellen shouted, "Crystal, it's all right, you'll be fine now."

"No..." she replied, her chest heaving with the effort it took to speak, "I won't be all right. It's too late."

"No! It's not too late!" cried Ellen, tears flowing freely down her face.

"It didn't hurt you, did it?" panted Crystal.

"No, I'm fine. And you will be, too! I've got a healing potion!"

"It would take too long to work. Don't worry, Ellen. I protected you, I've done my job," sighed Crystal, her breathing slowing.

"And I'll keep protecting you, I will. I won't let anything happen to you, or your friends, I promise."

"No, Crystal, don't do this to me!" cried Ellen, as her wings slowly started to fade into dragon dust.

"Goodbye, Ellen. You were the best Dragon Tamer I could ever have..." She said, closing her eyes and fading to dust with a small sigh.

"No, please, no..." sobbed Ellen, her tears falling upon the small pile and revealing something below it.

"Sam is she really..." whispered Maree.

"Yes" she confirmed.

"Then how come Ellen didn't get a game over?" asked Ceirin, as they left Ellen, silent and still, lying next to her dragon's remains. As she cried, she spotted the object underneath the dust and, shaking, picked it up. It was an amulet, gold and shining, with an amber stone in the middle.

"Thank you, Crystal. I don't know what this is, or why you want me to have it, but thank you," she whispered. "And I'm sorry, but... I can't go through this without you. I have to go back where it's safe, and where nothing bad will happen to me. Goodbye."

Chapter 12: *Return to the Valley*

"But you have to come with us! You have to play the game," said Nick.

"This is role playing. I'll do what I like, which is go back where it's safe."

"Look, I know we can't stop you going, but I don't think the game will work that way. We have to finish the game, we're the dragon tamers!" Maree said.

"How can I be without a dragon? All I am is a homesick newbie who accidentally ended up here. Without Crystal, I'm nothing but a glitch. I'm going back."

"If you go back, then at least let us take you there," suggested Nick.

"Come on then. Let's get you back," sighed Ceirin.

"We'll be quickest if we fly." Ellen said, taking the Phoenix Feather out of her backpack.

They all gathered round it, and there were murmurs of '*LinksofChain*'.

The flight upwards was a slow one, the group sad as they tried to think of what to do now, except for Ellen, who flew far ahead of the others, excited at the thought of returning to the safety of the Valley.

The rest of the tamers stayed huddled together, discussing between themselves what to do as they watched her. She stopped in mid air, and flew even quicker towards the ground.

"We must be almost there," said Sam. Maree didn't reply, she was too busy watching Ellen. She had turned, and was flying towards them.

"Help!" she cried as she came nearer. "The Valley's on fire!"

Everyone forgot about their worries and followed her. The amount of smoke was huge, billowing up into the air.

"Nick! Can't you do something? Turn into a giant fire blanket or something?" Ellen said, shaking as she flopped to the ground and lost her wings.

"Sorry, but there's no way. It's like stretching an elastic band; it can only go so far without either snapping or returning to its normal shape. Becoming a sheet in Serta was hard enough!"

"That fire's huge!" said Ceirin. "There's no way to put it out!"

"There might be...but we have to go to the pool. Come on!" said Maree, flying up again.

"Climb up, Ellen," said Sam, crouching down in front of Ellen. "We have to hurry."

"We can help too. Nick, turn into a dog." Ceirin said, picking up dog-Nick (who had turned into a husky puppy, just small enough for Ceirin to lift him) and flying after Maree. But the smoke was thick, choking him as he flew, and he soon lost all his sense of direction.

"Nick!" he spluttered. "I'm lost, the smoke's too thick!"

"Land, the smoke's not as bad at ground level," instructed Nick. They landed in the midst of the flames, black and sweating.

"Lie down, Ceirin, and try to relax. When I transform, climb on, and I'll try to fly above the smoke. The higher we get, the colder it'll become, but you can't fall off." Nick transformed into his eagle form, and Ceirin climbed on. He beat his wings, and the fire spread outwards as he rose. But as he entered the smoke, Ceirin started coughing, and he flew back down to the ground.

"Ceirin, you'll have to hold onto my feet, that way my wings should blow away the smoke from you." They repositioned themselves, and rose again.

This time Ceirin could breathe as he flew, but the cold wind caused by Nick's flapping blew him about as he held onto Nicks claws for dear life. They flew higher and higher, but still the smoke didn't clear. It kept on getting colder, and Ceirin's hands grew numb. Nick was even worse; a coating of frost had formed on his feathers. With each flap, Ceirin's grip grew weaker and Nick grew more worried.

Suddenly, they cleared the smoke, and could see plumes of water coming from where Sam was.

Nick turned and flew even faster, and Ceirin was flung violently, his hands slipping until he was hanging from only one.

Nick was trying to reach the ground before Ceirin fell, and failed to notice this.

He reached the pond area and stopped suddenly to stop him crashing, accidentally flinging Ceirin into the air.

Everyone had no choice but to watch in shock as he flew directly towards the roof of Sam's cave.

Chapter 13: *Fabrico, the secret world*

Ceirin closed his eyes and wondered what would happen. He was going to die, that was certain, but what would happen after that? But the impact wasn't what he expected. Instead of cold rock, he banged his head against something soft.

"Ouch! That hurt!" It shouted, and as Ceirin opened his eyes he wondered if he was seeing things. A large and angry toy dragon was pulling itself from under him.

"Thanks a bunch! First, I get kicked out of Fabrico, then I end up here, then the place catches fire, and to top it all off, some mad player lands on top of me."

"Fabrico? What's that?" Ceirin asked, looking in dismay at the parts of his body that hadn't landed on the toy.

"It's the hidden world, where all the toy dragons live," it said. "Why aren't you there?"

"I was banished." The toy said, its strange fabric turning slightly red.

"Wow! What did you do?" said Ceirin, imagining the little dragon running around with scissors and cutting up all the other toys.

"I...I...got caught in a corner and tore!" wailed the little creature, glassy tears rolling down from its glass eyes as it turned to reveal a tail that was hanging off.

Ceirin had never used a needle in his life. But he did like making machines, and he had imagined sewing to be like fiddling with the fine wires that made up machines.

"Well...I suppose I could try to sew you back together..." he said reluctantly.

"No need for that when there are girls here!" said Maree, climbing up to the top of the cave and throwing her arms around Ceirin. "I'm so glad you're alright!"

"How did it go?" he asked, blushing.

"Well, it didn't go so good. There was too little water to put it out...and my wings caught fire," she said, getting back up and also blushing.

"You should have seen it! Her hair nearly burned too, but the Phoenix wings disappeared and the flames went with them." Ellen said, climbing up with Sam behind her, and on her shoulder, Nick, in mouse form.

He saw Ceirin and bounded towards him as a wolf, bowling him over and licking him madly.

"So why are you out here" asked Maree.

"I got ripped, and was exiled from Fabrico, my home. Now, I have to go to the creator to get sewn back together. But he's changed. The last dragon that went there was...torn to pieces by the Destroyer!" If a toy could looked shocked, then the little plush creature certainly did.

"Oh my! There's no need to go there just to get sewn. Nick, a needle please," ordered Maree.

Nick transformed, reluctantly, and, after pulling out a strand of her own hair for thread, Maree quickly and neatly stitched Niko's tail back on.

"How do you girls do that?" asked Ceirin.

"Magic," Ellen replied with a grin.

"So Niko," Maree mumbled as she sewed. "What are you made of?"

"Dead dragon scales," Niko replied. Maree dropped the needle, pricking her finger as she picked up the wrong end.

"Dead dragon scales!" squeaked Needle-Nick.

"Of course. With all the dragons dying, it's a plentiful material, and a good way to recycle." Everyone looked taken back by this.

"Niko, take me to Fabrico," demanded Ellen, as Niko ran in circles happily testing out his repaired tail. She seemed to have completely forgotten about the valley.

"Follow me!" he cried, leaping down the path. "I'm going home!"

*   *   *

Fabrico was huge, with every building or house made from fabric, which made them lean sideways dangerously, and dragon toys peered out of clear scale windows.

As they passed through the world Niko pointed out everything to them.

"There's the town hall...the factory where scales are turned into anything...the washing machine..." They stopped and stared at the washing machine. It was huge, even to the humans, lying on its side and filled with water. Dragons of all ages laughed and swam in it happily as it span round. Other dragons struggled to carry bucket after bucket of washing powder to the tray, which yet more dragons were using as a beach. "

"You know, I wouldn't mind a swim..." said Ceirin.

"I wouldn't if I were you. You might end up like a sock...lost in the wash." Nick warned.

It was only after they'd toured the whole city, that they realised Ellen had gone.

*   *   *

The factory workers all stared at Ellen as she came in. They were humans! Real players! There were two of them at the door, one in a bullfighter outfit with a Minotaur-like dragon, another timid player with glasses and a mole-like dragon.

"What...you're players!" she exclaimed, coming through the door.

"What are you so amazed about?" Bullfighter asked.

"I thought the game was closed!"

"It is...but this area's got some bugs..." the timid one said.

Suddenly, the four disappeared, and then came back. "See what I mean?"

"Is there anywhere in this factory not affected?"

"No. You should leave, in case this area closes. It's done it a few times today," grunted the bull.

This frightened Ellen. None of the three tamers could leave the game. So what would happen if an area closed? Would she just disappear?

"I'm looking for a certain dragon skin. Where could I find it?" She asked, shaking away the thought.

"Why? And where's your dragon?" questioned the bullfighter.

"It's her skin!" Ellen replied quickly

"But that can't be right. You shouldn't still be in the game if you dragon's dead!" squeaked the mole.

80

"I know. It's strange. But I live a strange life."

"Then you'll be looking for something made from a strange skin, I suppose," concluded mole's tamer. "I know! The Strange Cloak! That one they made this morning." She ran off, and returned with a scale cloak. Ellen knew at once that it was Crystal's.

The collar was decorated with dragon crystal from her hooves and wing tips, and it was fastened using her horn, cleverly changed so that it clipped together.

It was tasselled with Crystal's mane and tail hair, and the cloak itself was made from her shining silver scales. Normally, it would have alarmed Ellen. But it was so beautiful...

"Try it on," said the girl, holding up a mirror. When it was on and she looked at it, she was shocked at how magical it looked.

"Now, wish you weren't here," she said. It was a strange request, but Ellen was grateful to the girl for finding her cloak, and did so. Her reflection disappeared.

"Was that the glitch?" asked Ellen as her reflection returned.

"No. The cloak has a strange power. It can blend in with the background so that you disappear. But it changes as you move, so that you seem completely invisible unless you touch someone." As she finished this, the girl started appearing and reappearing amazingly fast. "Hurry! Leave!" she cried, hurling Ellen out of the door.

Ellen turned back to utter a thank you, but when she looked round, the building had disappeared.

Realising her friends would be looking for her, she quickly thought '*I am a ghost, invisible to all*', and disappeared, then ran back to the group.

"Hey, where'd Ellen go?" asked Sam, looking around.

"I'm right here," she said, quickly stuffing the cloak into her bag.

"Did you hear? This road can lead us to a fire imp, who can tell us how to get back to Destro!" Maree said, pointing at a path leading out of Fabrico.

"Is Niko coming with us?" Ellen asked.

"No, he has to stay where he belongs. This is our quest, and we'll have to complete it on our own."

Chapter 14: *The Imp's Advice*

The path from Fabrico took them to a large volcanic mountain. They climbed for almost a day before reaching the summit, and with each step it grew hotter.

"I hope this volcano isn't still active, or else we're in trouble," said Ellen as they reached the top.

"We're in trouble," said Nick. He was tired, after shape shifting into all sorts of animals and dragons before settling on a mountain goat. He would have preferred being a bird, but had been too weak to change shape again. He was first to reach the top, and see the bubbling pool of lava not far below them. Needless to say, he quickly stepped away.

"Geesh...Lava...why does it *always* have to be lava! Some games are nothing but Lava! Before we know it, we'll be playing games like 'Lucky Lava's adventures in Lava Land!" moaned Ceirin.

"I know! And why have a *fire* imp. Because it's an excuse to have lava!" added Nick.

"So how do we get to the fire imp? Abseil down?" suggested Sam sarcastically. "Don't worry, there'll be a way!" Ellen said cheerfully.

"I'll try flying" said Nick, changing into a bluebird and flapping unsteadily down. "He looks pretty tired. He shouldn't have gone down," said Sam, as his flapping became slower. Suddenly, Nick stopped flapping and started to fall down.

"He can't fly any longer! yelled Ceirin, moving to go after Nick. Maree grabbed him before he could.

"Ceirin, jumping into an active volcano is not the clever thing to do," she sighed. "Sam, go help Nick!"

Sam dove into the volcano. She tried to catch him, but he kept sliding off, unconscious. Instead, she turned round in mid air and managed to snatch one of his wings in her teeth. Sweating, Sam flapped up, helped by the heat rising from the volcano. Then, she moved to the side and disappeared from view.

"Where's she gone?" asked Maree.

"It looks like some sort of passage. Use the Phoenix feather spell to follow her." Ellen pulled it out of her bag, and they all gathered round.

"*Linksofchain!*" they chanted."

"You'd think that feather would be tired out, the amount of times we use it!" said Ceirin as they grew. "We need to think up a more permanent solution...I wonder if they do plastic surgery here..."

"No way!" Ellen and Maree shouted together.

"Alright, alright, I was just joking..." he mumbled, avoiding their glares.

As soon as they flew down into the volcano they found the heat unbearable. A hot steam was everywhere, and it was hard to see anything.

"Was this steam here before we arrived?" asked Maree.

"No. Something must be causing it," observed Ceirin.

"It's a signal from Sam! she's blasting water down onto the lava!" shouted Ellen, hovering lower down. Her voice echoed around the volcano, and a fountain of water suddenly shot into the air.

"Follow the jet of water down. We should find her." Ellen called, diving down. The jet led them down into a small tunnel in the side of the volcano. It looked like a stream of lava once ran along it, but the lava had been blocked off when part of the tunnel collapsed. Now, new paths ran in all directions.

Sam was lying down there, panting, with Nick lying next to her still in bird form. He was soaking wet from Sam blasting him every so often, and still unconscious, but cool despite the heat in the volcano.

Maree and Ceirin landed and started fussing over them, leaving Ellen hovering uncertainly outside. While she watched, she noticed something moving behind them.

She landed on a small ledge that hung over the tunnel, and lost her wings. Then she pulled on her cloak, and climbed down to the tunnel with her gloves protecting her hands from the hot rock.

Invisible, she snuck behind the group and saw a small creature, made entirely of lava, watching intently from behind some rocks where the tunnel had collapsed.

She walked down a path nearby, and took off the cloak, before walking beside the creature.

"You must be the fire imp," she said.

"Where did you come from?" it yelped, jumping at her voice.

"We came to ask if you knew how to reach the last level."

"So that's what you want! You humans are mad! All that'll happen there is you'll get a game over!" he yelled. Ellen didn't reply, but instead stood, tapping her foot impatiently.

"But if that's what you want, I must oblige.... Gather your friends and follow me to my home. Your dragons should be able to rest there." he sighed eventually.

"Come on, everyone. This imps going to tell us how to reach the last level!" shouted Ellen.

Sam rose, helped by Maree, and Ceirin took Nick in his hands. Then they started to follow the imp as he led them deeper into the volcano.

"When the game was being made, strange things started to happen. The main one was a sudden change to the creator. He was always quite sad, but that was to be expected as he was the only human here. But he loved to be with the creatures he made. Then, quite suddenly, he became very withdrawn, and hid himself inside Destro.

He tried to make himself as best hidden as he could, so much so that the last level, his home, became impossible to enter. But game rules stated that the game had to have a solution. So he had to create items to bypass all his security systems. These he hid all over the game world, guarded by many of the characters. He even made one, the most powerful of all despite not being used to enter Destro, only obtainable by following certain steps, and doing something that would most certainly get you a game over before you received the items. That item is a secret, but the others are known," said the imp as they walked.

"To get past the snake guardian, you have to use a certain magical musical instrument, to charm the snake. There are portals to that

84

place all over the volcano, so we can help you get that. Then, Sonic Wings, to pass the 'Supersonic Speed Test'. Finally, a voice changer and some mirror lenses, to fool the voice and iris scanners." They had arrived at the bank of a huge lava river.

"How are we going to get over this?" asked Ceirin

"It's no trouble for me. I'm made of lava, I just swim through it. But I don't know how a human would get over," the Imp said, shrugging.

"We could always fly, with the Phoenix Wings," suggested Maree.

"It wouldn't work. With the ceiling this low, and the tunnel so small, the heat here is even worse than in the mouth of the volcano. You'd be exhausted before you reached the other side, and there would be too big a danger of you falling mid-flight."

Maree looked around. Ellen was walking towards the edge of the lava river. Out of hearing from the others, something was calling her…

"Ellen! Come over here! We must talk to you!"

If Ellen's mind had not been clouded, it would probably be screaming "Don't talk to strangers!" at her.

But it wasn't.

"Hurry! Come closer! We must see the amulet!"

The voice had taken on a tone of urgency. As it hung round her neck, the amulet glowed bright orange. Ellen leaned forward towards the lava.

Suddenly, out from it hurtled a head, screaming wildly, and after it a body. Yellow eyes and fangs glinted in the warm glow of the lava that dripped off its scaly back. It grabbed Ellen's neck, and tried to pull her under. She screamed as the hands, though icy cold, burnt into her skin.

Suddenly, another hand, a human one, grabbed her, and Maree's invisible sword, now glowing an even darker purple than it had against the Minotaur, whistled through the air.

As its hand, cut straight off, splashed into the lava, the creature dived down after them, without even leaving a ripple in the lava. Ellen gave a sigh of relief, rubbing her neck, but her breath quickly came once more in short gasps when she realised what was happening. A grey liquid had covered her legs and hardened, leaving her stuck to the ground. It was quickly spreading. Soon, Ellen would be nothing but an oddly-shaped rock.

"What do we do?" Maree yelled to the imp, her sword having no effect on the liquid. The fire imp was panicking, and started chanting some kind of spell.

"By the power of Yin and Yang, with which fire and water come together to produce these lava caves, home to all the fire imps, and the land all around, home to all others. I command all that disrupt the harmony of this place to vanish!" he yelled, placing his hand on the ground. It glowed red in response, and everyone standing on it disappeared.

*   *   *

When the opened their eyes, they were standing in what would have been a blank space, had it not been filled with broken images, rough, unfinished sketches and other various pieces of rubbish.

"Talk about a litter lout…Where in the world are we?" asked Ceirin, his voice echoing all around.

"Unfinished area of the site. No access." said Nick.

"How did you know that?" asked Ceirin. Nick held up a piece of Notepad paper.

"A piece of an old Notepad document. This place hasn't been updated in a while!" said Sam, blasting a jet of water at a cobweb that had been annoying her.

"How are we supposed to get out of here?" asked Ellen.

"Unless you happen to be able to perform imp magic, the only way out is down here," said the imp, opening a trap door. "Down here, you will find the magical musical instrument, along with the creatures that guard it."

"You really expect us to go down underwater! How are we supposed to breathe?" exclaimed Ceirin, still unsure about going into deep water.

"Your fishy friend there's a water element. Surely she has some sort of power to help you?" the imp replied. Sam glared at him.

"You're right!" said Maree. "If we all hold onto Sam, we'll be able to breathe underwater!"

"I don't know if I'm up to that...and I'm sure Nick isn't." Sam said uncertainly.

"You'll be able to rest when you get down. Now, please, leave!" cried the imp impatiently.

"Well, what have we got to lose?" cried Ceirin, jumping down.

*   *   *

The trapdoor was in the roof of a small cave, looking out onto a bright blue sea. Even in the shade it was boiling, and small lizards lay cooling in holes all over the cave. After Ceirin called up that it was safe, the rest of the group dropped down and looked around. Looking out, they saw a huge sun, larger than it was anywhere on Earth.

"Looks like Tropica, the tropical planet, to me," said Ceirin.

"How did you know that? Have you ever been here?" asked Ellen.

"No, never. Oh..." Ceirin only just realised what he'd said. It was confusing. He knew this place, but he had no memory of it at all. He'd never even been here.

"Come on, we better lie down," said Maree. Sam happily collapsed down, with Maree and Ellen following. Ceirin took longer, making a small bed for Nick in the corner. The bluebird was still unconscious, but slowly recovering.

By the time Ceirin lay down in his sleeping bag, everyone was fast asleep.

Chapter 15: *The Siren Cities*

When the tamers awoke, all the Dragons were already up before, staring up at the sky and murmuring to themselves.

"What's wrong everyone?" yawned Ellen.

"Good, you're awake. Come and see this, Ellen."

"What is it? All I see is water?"

"Look further up, look at the sun. Do you notice anything?"

"The Sun...what's happening to it?"

"It's getting closer at an alarming speed. This planet may not have much time left!" Called Nick, hawk-formed as he flew high in the air.

"We've been watching it since we rose. There's creatures here, I saw them while fishing in the morning, them seem afraid to go near the surface. I think they believe they'll be safe if they stay underwater." said Sam sadly.

"We have to go help them!" exclaimed Maree, lying awake in the corner.

"Five more minutes, mum..." mumbled Ceirin, pulling his pillow over his head.

"He's *still* sleeping!"

"Not for long he's not..." laughed Nick.

"Cover your ears!" cried Sam as she watched Nick transform into a huge foghorn. He blew, as hard as he could, causing rocks to fall from the ceiling.

"Not funny," moaned Ceirin, hiding under his sleeping bag from the avalanche. "A boy can't get a decent sleep around here."

"Well we need to start earlier if we're going to go down there," said Sam.

"You're not seriously thinking of going down underwater, are you?" exclaimed Ceirin. Too late, everyone remembered his fear of deep water. "I can't!"

"Of course you can Ceirin," soothed Maree.

"I'll be with you this time," added Nick, transforming into a puppy and looking up at Ceirin with big brown eyes.

"How am I meant to say no to a face like that?" laughed Ceirin, stroking Nick fondly on the head. "I'll do it."

The rest of that morning was spent making odd ropes out of seaweed, to help everyone hold on to Sam.

"Is this really worth the effort?" asked Maree.

"No. But I needed something to keep you busy."

"Those creatures you saw earlier...what were they?"

"Sirens." Sam whispered.

"Sirens!" Maree exclaimed, before Samantha quickly put her hand over Maree's mouth.

"She wanted to know what those things on top of ambulances were called." lied Sam to the others. "Look, Maree. Nick and I both don't want the others to find out. They might refuse to go," hissed Sam.

"But those things could kill them!" whispered Maree.

"We'll look after those two. Don't worry." reassured Sam.

"Lets go then. The ropes are ready," sighed Maree.

They dived down, each holding onto the strong seaweed Sam had chosen to use as ropes. It had large bubbles on it, acting as both grips and an air supply if needed.

They swam for hours, but the water seemed empty. No one knew how deep this water was, or how long it would take to reach the bottom.

Then, Nick, in dolphin form, spotted something large floating in the water. Huge, in fact. It looked like...buildings...a city under-water."

"Looks like we've found Atlantis." said Ceirin.

"I don't think that's Atlantis," said Sam. Creatures were coming from the city. They looked almost human.

"What are they?" asked Ellen.

"They look like girls. Other players maybe."

"We should go see them." Ellen said, swimming towards them with the seaweed rope behind her. Hesitantly, Maree followed.

"What are they doing?" asked Ceirin.

"Talking," replied Nick.

"Hello there. Are you players?" asked Ellen.

"Oh no. I'm afraid we're sirens," the nearest said.

"You look like humans," said Maree.

"You think so? I like this illusion in particular as well," it said.

"Illusion?"

"Yes. We don't really look like this. It's a trick we play on the males."

"We better not let Ceirin see you then." laughed Maree.

"Ceirin?"

"He's a boy from our group," explained Ellen.

"A boy you say. I must go meet him!" it shrieked.

"One of them is coming over," said Sam, watching the sirens.

"Hello there! Do you mind if I speak to Ceirin?" it called.

"N-No," stammered Ceirin, looking at the sirens in awe. "Not at all."

"Hello, Ceirin. My friends told me all about you, and you sounded so lovely that I just had to say hello. My name's Pearl."

"Ceirin, I don't trust her," hissed Sam.

"I was wondering if you'd like to come for a swim with me. Not far, of course, and you'd have your seaweed with you."

"I don't see why not," said Ceirin.

"Idiot!" cried Nick, as he started to swim away. "What's he doing?"

"Going for a swim with his new girlfriend, apparently," sighed Sam.

"Humans…" Nick and Sam sighed together.

Not far away, two male sirens had approached Maree and Ellen, and they were deep in conversation. The sirens kept asking them to move closer, away from Sam.

"I don't trust these things, Nick. You look after Ceirin; I'll look after the girls."

As they moved after them, however, the sirens all snapped the seaweed ropes behind the tamers back. The humans started cough and spluttering, trying to speak but now unable.

90

"No! Hurry Nick!" yelled Sam, rushing towards the girls as they floundered in the water. The Sirens saw them, and each grabbed a human, swimming off with them.

As they swam faster, they started to lose their ability to hide their true form – ugly creatures, with dull green scales with many missing or hanging off, round white eyes with large black pupils and red gills in their necks. Their teeth were oddly shark-like, though only the tamers were unfortunate enough to be able to see them. The longer they swam the less human and more frog-like the rest of their bodies became, and the faster they got.

Nick followed Ceirin as they took him towards the city, and Sam followed the girls and the male sirens heading in a different direction.

"Sam, we can't let them reach the city, they'll be too many!" shouted Nick as they separated.

"I know! Nick, try to mimic my shape. It might not work as well, but it may let you use my water-breathing ability. Now hurry!"

"And *why* didn't you tell me this before?" demanded Nick.

"Because I wanted to test it. I'm not sure if it will work. But we can try!"

Ahead of them, unsurprisingly, the tamers had passed out. Neither of the dragons were sure how long they could remain like that without drowning, and they didn't want to find out.

The sirens weren't tiring, and in Nick's case they were getting closer to the city.

How long can we keep this up, he thought. *These creatures aren't tiring. It's like making toddlers run against athletes.*

Then he remembered something Ceirin had told him a long time ago, when they had been training, trying to reach the place of most powerful Dragon in the realm.

They had been training all day, and Nick was exhausted. The wild dragons kept on coming, testing them, seeing if they'd be able to handle the pressure. Nick wasn't sure if he could anymore. If he failed...

But Ceirin was determined not to let him. He hadn't been playing for long, and was enjoying it. Every time Nick tried to give up, he

*would yell and cheer, coaxing him on, giving him all sorts of ideas
for new creatures to use. Nick truly couldn't fight anymore. His
head was spinning, his body weak, bruised and beaten.*

*Ceirin saw him staggering, and finally realised what a state Nick
was in. He didn't have a healing potion; he wasn't sure what he
could do. So he did the only thing he could, ran in front of Nick
and faced the wild dragon.*

*"What are you doing...if you fight; he'll be allowed to hurt you!"
gasped Nick.*

*"Of course I know that. But I have to protect you, you're my drag-
on," he said with a grin. "Anyway, you're not the only one being
tested. I have to be brave if I want to look after you, and I'm going
to!"*

*He had taken on that Dragon, and won. Then, he had picked up
Nick in mouse form, and ran away from them so that they couldn't
hurt him.*

"And I won't let them hurt you," said Nick to Ceirin, despite him
being unconscious. "I won't let them!"

"No! He's speeding up!" hissed the siren, as Nick got closer.

"Did you miss me?" asked Nick, laughing at the Siren's faces.

"You can't go that fast! It's impossible!"

"No, it's possible..." growled Nick. "Because I won't let anyone
hurt my tamer!" He shot forward, hitting the siren from the side at
full speed. Ceirin was knocked out of its grasp, and it sped away
from Nick, shouting something angrily in another language.

"Nick! There's something above you! Go there with Ceirin, and
I'll meet you there!" shouted Sam, much further away.

"Do you need help?"

"No! Something good is happening!" she replied.

Nick hurriedly grabbed Ceirin and swam up to the surface, aware
the Sam's ability was working, but only enough to stop Ceirin
from drowning completely.

Sam had directed him to a small island, with nothing on it but a
doorway with nothing behind it.

He sat outside there, trying to see what was going on below him,
with Ceirin quickly gaining consciousness next to him. He was

almost fully awake. Nick looked down and saw, to his shock, a large group of sirens swimming up to where they were.

"Wow. Ceirin sure is popular with the ladies..." said Nick sarcastically, before turning into a large Alsatian dog, heaving Ceirin onto his back, and running through the doorway.

When the sirens reached the waters surface, they found the island completely empty.

*　　　*　　　*

This is strange. Like when I was talking to Maree, but there's no one else talking. Why is it happening again? I don't need to talk to anyone now...except Crystal. But she's gone. There must be a reason.

Time? Why did she think that? No one said it, she just thought of it. Time? Was it some kind of riddle? What made her think that? Is there anyone else here? Hello? Answer me, please. Who are you?

When Ellen awoke, she was still underwater. She panicked, realising she wasn't holding onto Sam. But how was she still breathing?

"Ellen! You're breathing underwater!" exclaimed Sam, looking at her.

"I don't know how I'm doing it. I'm confused," said Ellen. She looked down, and saw that her amulet was throbbing violently. Surely it wasn't doing this...

"Ellen! Listen to me! You have to slow down the two Sirens!"

"How?" asked Ellen, before the siren carrying her started hissing something, and they accelerated away from Sam. Looking at it, she was disgusted. Something that looked so human not long ago had turned into this repulsive frog-fish monster.

Now it realised she was conscious, it started trying to knock her unconscious again. It placed its horrible, slimy hands over her face, suffocating her.

I never did like the taste of fish! thought Ellen as she bit down hard.

The creature made a noise, a loud chorus of blubbing, croaking, and other noises.

Something green oozed out of its hand, and it dropped Ellen and swam back, colliding with the Siren holding Maree.

"Yes!" yelled Sam, and started charging into the sirens. "Ellen, grab onto me. We have to try and find the power-up item." she added, grabbing Maree.

"I'll try to wake Maree up, so she can help!" added Ellen, swinging herself onto Sam rather like she did on Crystal. "Sam, I think we should go to the female siren city. They don't attack if you're the same gender!"

"That's a great idea! Let's go!" said Sam, turning round so sharply Ellen had to grab Maree to stop her falling off, and heading past the sirens to the first city.

"There's more of them coming after us!" yelled Maree, coming round and looking back to see more of the male sirens.

"And there's some at the island Nick went to!" added Ellen. "We're completely outnumbered!"

"But we're still going to try!" said Sam, grinning madly, and Maree realised she was enjoying herself. This was Sam's field, water, and nothing was going to stop her when she was in it.

"Ellen, get down. It will help Sam swim faster." said Maree, remembering when they used to see how fast they could swim, chasing after fish in the valley.

They sped through the water, past the groups of siren and into the city. It was a maze of stone passageways and crumbling walls, all covered in sea plants. They twisted and turned through the building, knocking over sirens and narrowly missing the walls.

They reached the only room left in the building that wasn't falling apart, some kind of music hall. Instruments were everywhere, but almost of all of them seemed cheap and easy to make, seaweed flutes, pebble xylophones, all manner of instruments either made from items in the sea, or from humans, most likely ones from the boats that crashed on the rocks.

One, however, stood apart from the rest. In the middle of the hall, on a small platform, lay an ocarina in a glass tank.

"Everyone, get down and close your eyes," shouted Sam urgently

94

as she headed towards the tank. "Maree, when the glass smashes, grab it," she instructed, slamming into it at full speed.

Glass flew everywhere, over Sam's scales and in Ellen and Maree's clothes and hair. Their faces were cut and scratched, as thousands of small shards of glass all came flying at them at once. It was like being caught in an underwater hail storm, but twice as painful.

In the middle of it all, Maree reached out to grab the ocarina. She missed, but managed to get the cord it was attached to, and pull it around her neck. It was heavy, and seemed to be made of something hard, most likely dragon crystal, as it was the most commonly used item in the game. It was covered in thousands of tiny scales, and also hundreds of small holes. Maree wondered how you were mean to know which ones to play.

Unable to slow down, Sam kept swimming, and went straight into one of the walls. Luckily, the stone was weak and badly eroded, and it was like swimming through a mixture of mud and sand.

The crowd of sirens was growing, and almost every siren in both the cities seemed to have joined the chase. But now there was a clear path to the island, and Sam turned sharply once more, went over and past the sirens below and underneath the island. Then she swam straight out, shooting up in the air like a rocket with Ellen and Maree clinging tightly on, before they tumbled onto the sand, through the doorway, and disappeared.

Chapter 16: *Mirror Lens Mission*

"Where are we Sam? And where did everyone else go?" asked Maree, staring at the trees that surrounded them.

"How am I meant to know that?" snapped Sam. "But, judging by all these trees, I'd say Berk, the woodland planet."

"This place has too many planets..." groaned Maree. "How are we meant to find the others? They could be anywhere; maybe that portal took them to a completely different planet!"

"Wherever they are, they can wait. I'm not going on another side quest, even dragons need a break!" moaned Sam.

"I can just tell this is going to be one of your bad days, Sam."

"Well it's not my fault. I've just flew down a volcano and nearly passed out, ran through a boiling tunnel, been transported to an unfinished area, then a planet that's about to collide with its own sun, and even been chased through the water by some angry frogs! I need a break! Fish isn't enough to keep a dragon going!"

"Sam, if you'd stop ranting and look around, you'd have realised we're being watched!" whispered Maree, taking her ocarina from around her neck.

Peering at them from the trees were hundreds of small beady eyes.

"What are they?" asked Samantha.

"I don't know, but they don't seem very friendly," said Maree, before a nut hit her on the nose. "Ow! Who threw that?" she demanded, and the creatures suddenly broke into a noisy chattering, and started throwing more nuts down.

"Oh, these things are asking for it!" growled Sam.

Maree raised the ocarina to her lips and blew a single note. The noise stopped, and the creatures watched Maree. She stared back, scanning the crowd. Then, she threw the ocarina at the nearest pair of eyes. There was an odd 'crack', and the creatures ran off, chattering angrily. Maree pulled back the ocarina by its cord, and

placed it back round her neck. A small red squirrel fell unconscious from the trees.

"It's a squirrel!" gasped Maree, staring at the animal, lying on the
ground with it's thick tail wrapped protectively around it.

"A what?" asked Sam, sniffing it cautiously.

"A squirrel. It's a creature from Earth," explained Maree.

"Is it edible?"

"Don't you dare! What did it ever do to you?"

"Made me hungry."

"That's not it's fault."

"Yes it is. Anyway, dragons are allowed to eat these things. In the
other planets, we eat fish when our tamers aren't here. So why
can't we eat squirrels?"

"Because I'm your tamer, and I say so!"

"Some dragons eat humans too..." muttered Sam under her breath.

"What was that?"

"I said, look, it's waking up," lied Sam. And, slowly, the little animal was waking up, and blinking groggily up at them. She put her
hand on its tail to stop it running away. "Can I eat it if it doesn't
do what it's told?"

"No!" squeaked the squirrel.

"Did I ask you?"

"No, but you asked about me."

"It has a point, you know," laughed Maree, watching Sam getting
wound up.

"How do you plan to stop me?" snarled Sam, baring her teeth.

"Ask nicely..." it whimpered.

"Leave it alone, Sam!" Maree said.

"Why should she?" it squeaked.

"Yeah, why should I?" said Sam, pouting as only a dragon could.

"Look," sighed Maree. "If you do what we tell you, we won't hurt
you."

"I'm not doing what you say!"

"So we'll hurt you!" grinned Sam.

"Don't hurt me!" it sobbed.

"This is getting us nowhere. This thing's trying to wind us up."

"So you'll let me free?" it suggested.

"No, I'll let Sam eat you!" shouted Maree angrily.

"Yes!" cried Sam, pouncing on the creature.

"Eeeeek! Alright! I'll tell you everything!" it shrieked.

"You heard it, Sam." Maree said, grinning.

"Awww…You humans never let us have any fun," moaned Sam, spitting out the bedraggled squirrel. "You were too furry anyway,"

"Now, tell us all you know about the power-up items," demanded Maree.

"And don't lie!" growled Sam.

"Oh, woe is me, having to reveal the greatest of the squirrel secrets!" it sobbed, while Sam and Maree sighed at its theatrics. "Every squirrel here knows about the mirror lenses, secret treasures for which many a squirrel has given his life."

"If that's what you want to do, feel free," muttered Sam sourly, as the squirrel took from his wet and rather squashed tail a small sphere, like a mirror ball, but about the size of a pinhead. He started whispering something, then twisting and turning it.

It started growing, until it was about the size of a human eye. Then, it split into two. The mirror lenses.

"Now will you let me go?"

"Of course we will …" maree paused.

"The name is Pine." Pine said angrily.

"Of course, Pine. You've been a great help, hasn't he Sam?"

"Yes, but I'm still hungry," said Sam under her breath, before replying. "Yes of course you have, fur ball. Now run before I change my mind about letting you go…" Reluctantly, Sam watched the creature run up the nearest tree, and leapt away.

"I knew this was one of your bad days." Maree sighed, looking at Sam.

"Good for you. But I'm still hungry."

"Have some nuts then. They're good for you!"

"You humans have something against me eating meat, don't you?"

"Not if it's coconut meat!" laughed Maree. "Now sit down and relax, Sam. You're too easy to wind up."

From above them, Pine stood, watching from a nearby tree. Beside him stood a group of friends and a large pile of old, hard nuts. Together, they took aim.

Chapter 17: *Ceirin in Konica*

"Ceirin, are you feeling alright?" asked Nick, as Ceirin lay panting on the ground.

"I'm fine Nick. That was just a bit too much water. I know I got over my fear at Fear Fork, but it's hard…"

"It's fine, Ceirin. You just take things at your own pace," coaxed Nick, wrapping around him in towel form.

"Nick…I'm sorry about what I'm doing, I really am. I wish I had another choice."

"So do I. But this is our only chance, we have to do it."

"I don't want to hurt them. What if they get killed?"

"I don't want to either. Maybe they'll just have a Memory Wipe"

"I hope so, Nick. I really do," sighed Ceirin. "Where are we now?"

"How am I supposed to know? I'm not an atlas!"

"So why don't you turn into one?"

"Good point," said Nick, turning into a map of the Dragon Realms. On an area marked Konica, a red light was flashing, with the words 'You Are Here' below it.

"Konica? Isn't that the area the rulebook doesn't have any information on?" asked Ceirin.

"Yes. I wonder why they couldn't get any information on it."

"You don't think he'd send me anywhere dangerous, do you?"

"Ceirin, you know him well enough by now. The only reason he hasn't killed you is because he needs you."

"You don't think he'd kill me, do you?"

"I think he would, if he had no further use for you."

"Maybe he's trying to get rid of me by sending me here." Ceirin felt sick at the thought.

"Don't worry; we can handle whatever he throws at us."

"I hope you're right. Maybe we should have a look round here, and find out what's on this planet. Maybe the others are here too."

"Don't count on it. We're weaker apart; he'll use that to his advantage."

They walked around the planet for hours, eventually losing all sense of direction. Everything was the same, grey. Grey sky, grey ground, it was like being trapped in a grey box.

"I hate this place," said Ceirin after a while.

"Yes. Everything's the same. It's depressing. Maybe this planet is designed to mess with your mind like that."

"If it is, then it's working," sighed Ceirin, sitting down.

"Don't be like that, Ceirin. You can't let this place bring you down," said Nick cheerily, in the form of a robin.

"Too late Nick. This place makes me feel so sad." Ceirin sighed, collapsing to the floor.

"Ceirin!" cried Nick, changing to a Phoenix and flying towards him.

Ceirin got up and sat still, his eyes clouded.

"What's wrong with you?" gasped Nick.

"I wonder how he's going to kill us..." muttered Ceirin.

"Don't think like that!"

"Maybe it'll be quick. Have we done enough for that?"

"Stop it!"

"Probably slow. Slow and painful. He'd enjoy that."

"Snap out of it!" roared Nick, transforming into a lion.

"Maybe it would be better if I died here, alone..."

"No!" roared Nick, leaping at Ceirin.

Ceirin, lying still with lion-Nick on top of him, felt something wet fall on him. Looking up, he saw that Nick was crying.

"You're not! You're not alone Ceirin. I'm here! I'm here for you."

"Nick..." whispered Ceirin, coming out of his daze.

"You're my tamer. And I promise I won't let anything happen to you," he sobbed.

"Oh Nick...I...I'm sorry..." Ceirin said, as Nick lifted his paws off his chest. He stood up, and threw his arms round the lion's neck, burying his face in his fur.

"Sam, Crystal and I. We only have one purpose, and that's to protect you. Crystal gave up her own life for Ellen, and Sam and I

100

would do the same! I won't just sit here and watch bad things happen to you!" Nick growled.

As he spoke, the area started to change. The ground began to creak and groan, and creatures stared rising from it. Strange creatures, with grey masks for faces, grey cloaks, strange bumpy bodies that didn't seem human, and small black eyes, like beads.

"What are those monsters…?" Ceirin asked, looking round.

"The creatures that live here," whimpered Nick, turning into a kitten.

"Nick, I need a weapon," said Ceirin.

"Are you sure you can defeat these things?"

"I can try, can't I?" grinned Ceirin, as Nick transformed into a long white spear, with a dragon crystal head. "Let's do this." He thrust the spear forward at one of the creatures.

"It went straight through!" exclaimed Ceirin, as Nick transformed into a bear and came shambling back.

He stooped down and picked up a stone from the ground, and threw it at another of the things. It landed not far in front of it. The creature made an odd gurgling sound, like laughter, and slithered over the stone, enveloping it. When it moved away, the stone had gone.

"Nick, how are we meant to defeat these things?"

"I'm not sure. Nothing seems to work on them."

"Do you think we were sent here to be defeated?" Nick didn't answer.

"Well, if we're going down, then we'll go down fighting," he said. Nick transformed into a rhino next to him, and they ran with all their might into the creatures. It was…strange, like trying to walk through jelly. The grey mass was everywhere, sticky and suffocating, slowing their movement.

They tried to walk through the mass, feeling it fill their noses and mouths, stopping them from breathing. As the air stopped reaching his lungs, Ceirin noticed something in the middle of the mass. A silver chip, floating in the greyness.

Beside him, Nick had changed from a rhino to a dog, and had stopped moving.

The grey mass was throbbing violently, and Ceirin heard all the creatures gurgling in unison.

He couldn't move his legs, and his lungs screaming for air. He was in such pain, and he could see from Nick's eyes that he was in pain too.

As a familiar blackness appeared in his vision, he reached out and grabbed the chip.

You can't defeat me, he thought as his hand closed round the tiny chip. *I won't die like this. I'm a Dragon Tamer.*

Chapter 18: *Ellen's Adventure*

When Ellen stepped through the portal, she found herself in complete darkness, and, even more alarmingly, falling through the air. Trying in vain to stop her descent, she pulled her bag off her back and pulled out the Phoenix Feather.

Worrying about how far away the ground was, she screamed '*LinksofChain*' and gave a sigh of relief when the wings sprouted from her back, and she finally stopped falling.

"That was close..." she gasped, hovering in the air while she waited for her heart to stop racing. While she was hovering, she felt an odd presence. Something was watching her. Looking round, she spotted a pair of yellow eyes staring back at her.

"Don't look so frightened, human," hissed a voice.

"I'm not afraid of anything!" lied Ellen.

"Don't be stupid. It's shown all over your face."

"You can't see my face."

"Oh, yes I can. You have discovered the planet of Dite, planet of darkness and touch light, home to the Kitecats."

"Touch Lights? Kitecats?"

"Kitecats, the cross between the Kite bird, and a feline."

"A cat?"

"Perhaps. Or I could be a lion, or a leopard, or a cheetah. Your life could be in grave danger. How would you know?" purred the voice.

"I'm not afraid of any of those."

"Well then you should be, for you are about to enter a city full of all of these, and more. All the felines from your world and many others. And who knows how many of them will be hungry."

"I'm looking for the power-up item," said Ellen. This strange creature was alarming her. She didn't know what its motives were, and she didn't want to find out.

103

"We have one, but you have no chance of getting them. We have the Sonic wings, and they are guarded by the toughest of all the Kitecats. If you wish to live, you should leave now. They could kill you as easily as a sleeping sparrow."

"I'll risk my chances," said Ellen coolly.

"Then you are a fool." it said angrily.

"Or maybe I'm a genius."

"Whatever you are, you will soon be dead." it hissed in disgust, flying ahead of her.

Ellen had arrived. In front of her was a path leading to a huge, temple-like building. Everything was illuminated by touch lights, with kitecats of all kinds swooping back and fore to switch them on.

They were strange creatures. Leopards, cheetahs, cats, tigers, lions, every feline on Earth and others from different planets, all with kite wings, in a range of sizes to fit the animal. Some walked on two legs, while others walked on four.

They all stared as she walked past, and Ellen felt uneasy. If only Crystal was here to protect her...she felt so alone without her, and so weak and vulnerable. She would have been happier if she had got a game over with Crystal, instead of being stuck in this game. Still, without anything or anyone to protect her, it wouldn't be long until she got one. She approached the temple, sure the power-up would be in their but unsure how to get them.

She decided to pause for a break, and set out her sleeping bag in a small opening at the side of the temple, hidden from the kitecats. What should she do? She could go in and ask, but what if they attacked?

As she lay in that area, she noticed a loud flapping noise nearby. Something was coming. Throwing the sleeping bag back into her bag, she flattened herself against the wall, trying to be as silent as was possible. The kitecat wasn't leaving, the flapping was getting closer.

Suddenly, all the touch lights went out, and the temple was left in darkness. The flapping stopped, and was replaced by the patting of feet along the stone.

Ellen gasped, as something passed outside the tunnel. It turned, and a pair of yellow eyes entered. Ellen turned, and tried to run, finding only walls. Trapped.

As she stood frozen, the kitecat raised a paw and covered her mouth, stopping her from screaming. Her head was pushed against the wall, and a deep voice echoed throughout the tunnel.

"Where is your dragon? Tell me, and you have a better chance of living," it said, raising its paw from her mouth and instead placing it against her chest.

"I don't have one," panted Ellen.

"Liar! You must, or else you would not be in the game!" it shouted, pressing harder.

"If I had one, it would help me…"

"We shall see. If your dragon does not come out, you shall be crushed." It roared, pressing so hard Ellen couldn't breathe. "Will your dragon let you die?"

Despite everything, Ellen laughed. She was going to see Crystal…because Crystal wasn't with her. Funny, in an ironic kind of way.

"Why are you laughing?" snarled the animal, not pressing as hard anymore.

"Because I'm going to see Crystal." Ellen giggled, as she fell to the ground.

*　　　*　　　*

Flying…she was flying. On Crystal? Something round her waist. Teeth? Crystal didn't have teeth that big.

The creature…was it eating her? It didn't hurt. Could it be…carrying her?

Voices…what were they saying? Maybe they knew. Could they take her to Crystal?

"What have you done now?" she didn't recognize that voice.

"There was a human hiding outside the building." That was the creature's voice. It sounded strange, with her in it's mouth.

"And what have you done to her?"

"I-I thought she had a dragon with her!"

105

"And she didn't?"

"No, none came to save her."

"So you killed her?!" The new animal seemed angry.
"I thought her Dragon would save her! She's meant to have one!"

"You killed a human girl without a dragon! Have you no shame?"

"She's not dead yet. Just unconscious. She keeps murmuring something about a crystal."

"Maybe it's her dragon, and they got lost. Poor thing."

"She's a human!" sighed the creature carrying her. "I should have just eaten her..."

"Don't you dare eat a human that's still alive, you cruel kitecat!"

"So can I eat it if I kill it? I'm hungry!" said the voice, and Ellen felt its jaws clamp down tighter. She gulped.

"No, you have to give it some sort of chance. If you're so desperate to eat it, do it fairly. Beat her in a challenge or something."

"You call that fair? I'd win easily!"

"At least the poor thing would have a chance! You leapt on it, in the dark, without even giving it a chance to defend itself! Now quiet, the human's waking."

"Can I eat it before it wakes? It'll be more bother if you let it wake up!"

"All you think about is food. Then again, so do most of the kitecats in this city. Now put it down, I wouldn't like to wake up to a face like yours."

Ellen was dropped down onto something soft – her sleeping bag. Not knowing what she'd see, she opened her eyes, and saw something so frightening she nearly fainted again.

In front of her was a huge lioness, and beside it an even larger lion, the creature that had attacked her. The lioness was looking at her sympathetically, while the lion was busy thinking about something.

"Feeling better, dear?" asked the lioness. "We are sorry about what happened, aren't we honey," she asked the lion. "I said, *aren't we honey*." She repeated, kicking the lion with her back leg.

"Oh! Um...yes, very sorry." it muttered with a grin that showed all its teeth.

106

"Can I go? I need to find the power-up item here."

"You want the Sonic Wings!" growled the lion.

"Oh, no, that's not a very good idea. You see, my husband guards them-"

"On the contrary, I think it's an excellent idea." interrupted the lion. "But, as much as I want to, I can't just give them to you. We'd have to do a little challenge. If you win, you get the wings."

"What if I lose?"

"Then...well, let's make it a surprise, eh?" It said smoothly.

"What if I don't want to do the challenge?" asked Ellen.

"Oh, I'm afraid you have to. We couldn't be sure you wouldn't try and steal it if we let you go."

"What's the challenge?"

"A simple dive down a cliff. Fastest wins."

"I won't do this challenge." Ellen said firmly.

"Oh you will. After all, you want to keep that lovely necklace, don't you?" grinned the lion, trying to yank it from her neck. Instantly, it tightened. The lion growled, and tried again. It got tighter, digging into Ellen's skin. He kept trying, and the necklace got tighter and tighter around Ellen's neck.

"Stop it, dear! Leave the necklace alone!" panicked the lioness.

"If the amulet won't come off, I'll just take her whole head off!" roared the kitecat.

As Ellen ran for the door, the amulet loosening, the lioness stepped in front of it, wings spread wide. The force of her opening her huge wings knocked Ellen off her feet, and she heard the lion growling behind her. She searched through her backpack for a weapon, anything at all. Then, she realised something. She turned round and faced the lion.

"Run," he growled. "It'll be more fun to catch you."

"You can't hurt me," replied Ellen.

"I can and I will."

"Try it," challenged Ellen.

And, together, the two lions pounced.

From her backpack, she brought out the dragon tamers rulebook, and as the two lions saw it, they remembered something. A rule long forgotten by the kitecats. They couldn't harm a human.

As the lions fell on Ellen, tearing at her with their claws, the game stayed true to its rules, and the lions slowly disappeared into a cloud of dragon dust.

Outside, the touch lights started flickering on and off, and the rest of the city realised what was happening.

Ellen raced out of the lion's den, into the heart of the temple. Kitecats were everywhere, trying to find out what was wrong. Ellen heard cries telling them to protect the wings, and she ran after the crowds heading to the temple, ducking underneath them as they flew past.

She entered a room with the power-ups in the middle, and grabbed them.

Then the game decided it was time.

There was a moment of confusion, when Ellen, Nick, Sam, Maree and Ceirin swapped places rapidly, before everyone found themselves lying in the middle of Destro's gardens.

Maree and Sam were bruised, from being pelted with nuts by Pine's friends. Ceirin was lying shaking; his fist clenched, with Nick beside him unconscious, both covered in the grey mass. Ellen was lying clutching a metal, wing-shaped badge, the Sonic Wings unused form, her clothes torn and ripped and a red circle around her neck.

"They didn't get us," panted Ceirin.

"Yes," agreed Ellen with a grin. "They didn't get us."

Chapter 19: *The Destroyer's Domain*

For almost half of that day, they rested, recovering from their ordeals. A Kilimario came from the Dragon Council, with a message and some healing potions.

Dear Dragon Tamers

You've finally reached the final level, with all the items required to enter. It's the time we've all been waiting for, the downfall of the Destroyer. But we have to warn you about something.
We cannot say much, or else we shall be removed from the game, but the Destroyer's Domain contains many secrets, and some of them you will not want to find out.
The Kilimario delivering this should also bring some healing potions, as we fear what you have been through may have injured some.
As much a burden though it is, the whole of the Dragon Realm is depending on you to do something every creature in this game wants to do, but none are able.
Good Luck

- The Dragon Council

"It's good to know someone's watching out for us," said Ceirin, bringing one of the potions to Nick.
The rest were shared out among the group, and before long they had completely healed.
While they were eating, they told each other all that had happened.
"So, what did the squirrel taste like, anyway?" asked Nick.
"I didn't get a chance to find out," moaned Sam.

"Those humans have no idea what they're messing with, do they?" sighed Nick.

"It's strange…if you have a dragon, the rules don't really count, and you can be attacked even if you don't fight. But if you don't, you're completely protected," mused Ceirin, as the tamers talked away from the dragons.

"Completely protected? I wish! If I was, that lion wouldn't have tried to chew me when he was carrying me!"

"You're right. The rules only seem to work in situations where you'll get a game over if they don't. But still, I suppose if they didn't the game wouldn't be any fun," added Maree.

"Has anyone been counting the number of times things have tried to kill us? If I did, I'd probably lose track!" laughed Ceirin.

"There's been kelpies, spiked cages, clear cages, mad Kilimario, wild dragons, falcons, giant spiders, sirens, grey blobs, kitecats, have I missed anything?"

"Don't forget my pet dog!" added Maree.

"What's your pet dog got to do with this?"

"Some day, I'll have time to tell you. But we have to go save the realm at some point, why not now?"

"Because there's a giant snake guarding the way, perhaps," suggested Sam sarcastically.

"Don't worry, I'll figure out how to use this thing to get past him," reassured Maree, looking at the Ocarina.

"I don't think throwing it at him will work," laughed Nick.

"I meant I'll play it!" said Maree, blushing.

"Whatever you say, squirrel-killer," muttered Sam.

"I didn't kill it!"

"No, but I wish you did. I'm still hungry."

"Then go eat some grass."

"I'm not a rabbit!" exclaimed Sam.

"Then you're a hare."

"I'd call this a cat fight, but it doesn't seem right when it's a girl and a dragon," sighed Ceirin. Nick nodded.

"Do you think they'll hurt each other?" asked Nick.

"Sam might. She's hungry, after all," giggled Ellen.

"I've never met a more quarrelsome pair," sighed Ceirin.

"I don't know. You and Nick are good at fighting," pointed out Ellen.

"Hey Ceirin! For the record, I'm not a kitty or your bathroom." Nick said angrily.

"What are you on about, Nick?" asked Ceirin, confused.

"You may never know," teased Nick.

"You were a kitty when we were in Konica, though." Ceirin said laughing.

"That was an accident! I hate cats!"

"Whatever you say, Nick…"

"We should get the Destroyer in a fight with Maree and Sam. It wouldn't stand a chance," said Ellen, watching the battle.

"So you think I can't get that Snake?" demanded Maree.

"What if I do?"

"Then I'll show you!" yelled Maree, storming off.

"Everyone, Maree's going to try and bewitch the snake. We should be ready in case she hurts herself," suggested Ellen, following Maree. "Did we keep one of those potions?"

"Should we have?" asked Nick nervously.

"Yeah, if we don't want to get killed by the Destroyer!" Ellen said angrily.

"Don't worry, it would take too long to work, anyway," soothed Ceirin.

"In case you've forgotten, Maree's about to take on King Slithers." Reminded Sam. Everyone quickly ran after Maree.

"Look, everyone, I can do this. Stay behind the gate, unless I tell you to come," demanded Maree. "Promise me you will."

"But-" started Sam.

"*Promise?*" There were mumbled agreements from the group.

"Right. Wish me luck," she said, marching through the gates. The Snake Guardian was lying down again, pretending to be asleep.

"Hey there, you big worm! Ready for another round?" yelled Maree.

"She's gone mad, hasn't she?" asked Ceirin.

"Give her time." replied Sam.

"You again! Where are your comradesssssssssssss? Die in Fear Fork, did they?" It hissed with glee.

"Actually, no. But I wanted a one-on-one showdown with you." Painfully aware as she said it that one of the group had died. Outside the gates, Ellen was thinking the same, and wishing she could show that snake what she thought of it. But she was saving her anger.

"Then you are a fool. Are you trying to be killed?" laughed the guardian.

"No. And I don't believe you can kill me."

"You're right, I cannot," it mused.

"Then I'll make it a fair one. I, Maree, player promise that you can hurt me and the rule won't be allowed to take effect."

"You're right...she has gone mad," sighed Sam.

"What isssssssss wrong with you?! Ississsssss sssssssssomething controlling you?" asked the confused Snake. "It wouldn't be a fair fight if there wassssssss."

"You care a lot about having a fair fight, don't you?" asked Maree.

"Yesssssss. What isssssssss the ussssssse in cheating when I'm going to win anyway? I won't let you think you could have lived if I played fair when you die."

"Pretty noble. Maybe I won't kill you."

"You have no chance againsssssst me! Why do you talk like you can do ssssssssssuch a thing?"

"Because I can. Now, before we fight, I must know one thing. Were you told to take us to Fear Fork, or did you do it of your own free will?"

"I did asssssssssss my masssssssssssster commanded."

"Thank you. Now, will you fight me?" Maree asked. It wasn't the Guardian's fault.

"Yessssss. But I am ssssssslightly sssssssssssssory you could not live. You are a sssssssssstrange tamer." it said, easily catching her with one of its tails.

"Sleep well, brave guardian." Maree said, raising her ocarina to her lips. Somehow, her fingers knew which holes to cover and what tune to play, and she found herself playing a strange, haunting melody.

"No! It can....it canno...it cannot...be..." the snake hissed as she played, it's eyes growing heavy, it's tails drooping. Gradually, it's grip loosened and it's tail fell, until Maree simply walked out.

"What do you know. You're not *completely* mad after all!" cheered Sam.

"What are you implying?" asked Maree.

"Come on you two!" interrupted Ellen. " Save your bickering until after we save the realm, alright?"

"What was all that about?" Ceirin asked, looking at Maree.

"The Guardian only did as it was commanded. It should die because of that." Maree explained.

They walked past the snake, through to an area they hadn't seen before. A huge castle with stones that looked like metal in the light, and which sparkled in the bright sunlight, sitting on top of a huge black cloud, as if suspended in mid air.

As they landed, Maree slipped the mirror lenses into her eyes. Into view came a network of laser beams, spread across the floor like a net. Beside her, Ceirin fitted the tiny metal sound wave mirroring machine onto his throat.

Stepping gingerly over the lasers, Maree stepped up to the door. Out of the wall came a pair of small, cup-shaped instruments, which attached themselves to Maree's eyes. She could feel the mirror lenses vibrating softly as the instruments copied the last eye scanned and projected it to the machine.

As Maree stood there, hoping the last person the machine had scanned was the creator of the game, she wondered just how this was working. If this was just a game, then how come she could feel the lenses in her eyes, how come everything seemed so real, how come Ellen was so sad...?

The machine pulled away, and Maree glanced at Ellen. She was staring blankly back, still and lifeless, and Maree felt a shiver run down her spine.

"Scan complete. You may enter." bleeped the machine after a pause. Ceirin was about to follow Maree through another gateway to the next area.

"Be careful. The last area had lasers on the ground," Sam warned. Ceirin pulled out his PDA and scanned the floor, as if looking to see where they were.

"Drat...Pressure Sensitive!" he said. Nick transformed into a magic carpet, and Ceirin hovered over to Maree. With him came Sam, looking awkward crouched down on the carpet. When they reached Maree, she and Ceirin quickly switched places, and Ceirin went towards the second door, solid, shiny metal, like the last one.

"Let's hope the imp was right about the voice test being next!" he exclaimed laughing, but Maree could see he was nervous. The castle floor was set in an odd pattern of squares, and he knew that if he was denied access one of these squares would open and he would fall to the ground. He gulped. It was a long way down...

Ceirin stepped up to the door. Two more instruments appeared. One pressed itself against Ceirin's throat, almost crushing the small metal wave changer, another just in front of his mouth.

"I am the tamer of the Destroyer. Let me enter!" Ceirin found himself demanding the machine, his voice quiet and sad. Behind him, Maree punched the air happily. The last person to arrive here was the destroyer's tamer! They would be able to enter. That is, if they could pass the speed test. It hadn't been at the start, so it must be now.

The instrument disappeared, and was replaced by a large screen showing a smiley face, that started talking away, greeting him, asking him how he was, and generally being awkward. Ceirin turned down its volume and ignored it.

The door sprang open, revealing a flashing runway. Above it, a sign said 'Supersonic Speed Test'.

"Supersonic speed? How are we meant to go that fast!" exclaimed Ceirin.

"We don't." said Ellen, startling Ceirin and Maree. "I do." From out of her bag, she pulled a small metal badge depicting a wing, her power up from Dite. They grew into two large wings, which she attached to her arms. They tilted slightly to the side as Ellen walked up to the runway. "I was wondering what these things

114

would be used for…"

"Do you wish to test your speed?" asked a voice.

"Yes," said Ellen firmly.

"You may start," said the Voice. For a second, Ellen seemed to flicker.

"You have passed!" said the Voice.

"What?!" exclaimed Ceirin. "She didn't even do anything!"

"Yes I did. I used the Sonic Wings to move faster than the eye can see." explained Ellen. Then she returned to the group, and became, once more, silent, with a blank expression on her face.

The doors opened, and the Dragon Tamers finally entered the Destroyer's Domain, the last level of the game…

Chapter 20: *Separation*

Inside, a young boy stood, probably around the age of thirteen. He was pale and skinny, with blonde hair and bright blue eyes. He was lying in a shaded corner of the building, on top of some cages. He looked like some kind of cross between a cat, boy and a vampire. He was wearing a motorcyclist's clothing, but didn't look as if he had been outside, let alone riding a motorcycle, in a long time.

"You're the Creator!?" exclaimed Ceirin.

"Yes. I suppose you are surprised that such a young boy could create such a marvellous world..." he said, boastfully. "I would tell you more, but that would be such a waste of time. Let's just get started with this battle, shall we? I warn you, I like to play dirty..." He grinned slyly, getting up and pulling out a remote. He pushed one of its many buttons, and the cage doors opened.

"A little group of wild Dragons I caught," he said, still grinning, "They hate Dragons that have been tamed by humans, and they hate humans themselves. In fact, since it's my game, I think I'll allow them to attack humans!" His grin grew slightly wider. Out of the doors came a group of dragons, one for each element.

"We can take them!" said Nick, growling. He transformed into a Border Collie dog, and pawed the ground, whining impatiently.

"Hmmm...I wouldn't want to waste our strength, maybe there's another way..." said Ceirin, thinking hard. "Got it! He won't be expecting this!" As the dragons came forward, he called out.

"Hi there, Dragons! I know you don't like humans, but why start on us? The player who's had you trapped in those cages for so long is just up there! Why don't you jump up, or fly up, and destroy him first? You're allowed to, the rules telling you not to

116

have been disabled!" he called, talking as naturally as he would to Maree, Sam or Nick.

The group changed direction, flying and leaping onto the roof. The boy's smile disappeared, as he scrabbled into a corner.

"So that's how you want to play, huh? Well guess what, I have more tricks up my sleeves than you could ever imagine..." He hissed, clapping his hands together. The Dragons disappeared in columns of light, and he along with them.

"That kids freaky..." said Ceirin.

"Yeah...he doesn't even look human!" commented Maree, nodding.

"Let's go catch up with the coward. I'll bet you he went along one of those corridors, they're the only ways out!" he said, running forward.

The stone corridors were built inside the walls of the building, and were small and cramped. Maree felt herself start to hyperventilate. Luckily, the corridor got wider as she walked along, and her breathing calmed down once more.

Ellen followed, silent as a ghost. She knew they had forgotten she was there. That was fine with her. She didn't want to be noticed.

The path forked out into three. Maree took the left one, Ceirin the middle one and Ellen the right-hand path. She jumped without thinking over the trapdoor, illuminated in the dark tunnel by her amulet. Maree and Ceirin weren't so lucky. They fell down, deeper and deeper into the darkness.

Not listening to their cries, Ellen just kept on walking. She had to talk to that boy.

The corridor opened out into a large room, empty apart from the boy, standing in the corner. She had to ask him something.

"Are you really the creator of this game?" she asked.

"Yes and No." he said.

"That's not an answer. More importantly, can you change the rules of the game?" Ellen pressed on.

"Ah! I know what you want! You think I'll change the rules to bring back your dragon. Think again." His voice was cold and emotionless.

"That's not all I want to know. What was Fear Fork doing in the game? I looked it up on Ceirin's PDA, after that guardian said it was a special punishment. It was not, and has never been part of the game. What was it doing there?" Her voice was just as cold and emotionless, but also demanding.

"You really want to know? I put it in. I designed it to stop all of you, but instead it only managed to kill a single dragon. You even, against all odds, survived. But still, one death is better than none!" He laughed, a hollow, empty laugh.

"You did this! You'll pay!" Ellen shouted.

"Why should I pay? It's not my fault, is it?"

"Of course it's your fault. You set it all up!"

"Yes, but it wasn't me who failed to get over her fears and stand up to that spider. It wasn't me who forced my dragon to try and save me. It wasn't me who killed Crystal. It was you!"

"You're wrong. I would never have hurt my own dragon."

"Oh, but you did..." The boy hissed. "You caused her death, the stupid, idiotic beginner that you are. You never should have been a tamer!" he cried.

"It wasn't my fault..." she whimpered.

"Kill her." He commanded to the Destroyer.

The Destroyer was, in fact, a robot. D-1 iZ, nicknamed 'Izzy', designed to look, think, and act like a human. But he had been changed from his original design, into a fighting machine. Unnatural strength, speed, power, and a skill for using any weapon, made him an unbeatable foe. On his chest was the claw mark, the sign left whenever an attack was made by him or the creatures he commanded.

His hands were his weapons, not only could they strangle and claw, but they could be changed into any weapon they had the parts for: guns, swords, daggers, and crossbows, if he didn't have a weapon he would find out how to get it.

"And don't forget to take her amulet when you do so," added the boy, his master.

"Quick or slow?" questioned the robot.

"Slow. Slow and as painful as you can make it." ordered the boy, his eyes shining at the thought of it. He would have liked to see her die, but he had more victims waiting.

*   *   *

In the left-hand corridor, Maree and Sam had also reached the end. The trapdoor had led them deeper into another tunnel, up spiral staircases and along winding corridors, until eventually they had reached the very top of the castle.

The boy was also in there, the same cold smile, the same pale face. "What trick have you got this time? Or are you finally going to stop with the tricks and fight like a true tamer?" said Sam with a sneer.

"Careful, Sam!" whispered Maree. She was scared. What if this boy could do to Sam what he did to those wild dragons? She would never forgive herself...

"What do you know? The brave little tamer has a weak spot...her Dragon. How Cute," mocked the boy.

"Are you really the creator? An evil little boy able to create a whole world? A creator who destroys his members? A final level blocked from players? This can't all be true. In fact, I'm starting to doubt any of it is!" questioned Maree, quickly changing the subject.

"You want to know the truth do you? You probably won't like it. In fact, I'm sure you won't." Maree was badly tempted to wipe the smile off that kid's face.

"Bring it on!" challenged Sam, bearing her teeth.

"This level is out of bounds because no one is allowed to find out my secret. If they do, they'll have to be destroyed. Do you want to find out, Maree. If you don't, you can go, a quick memory wipe and you'll be allowed to stay alive." She didn't move. There was no way she'd turn back, forgetting about all her friends and family, all the adventures she'd had.

"Fine then! I'm not the creator. I'm just using his body for a little while. He won't be able to use it again when I've finished, but, hey, he's just one human out of a million others, worthless. But I'm one in a million. I didn't choose to be here. I'm just a spirit, a

119

spirit of something so terrible I had to be removed from my world, stripped of any power so that I couldn't harm others, trapped inside a video game that was in the middle of being finished and which everyone thought would never be popular. Then, as it neared completion, it became a virtual reality game. The fools that trapped me here never though something like that would happen."

"So how could that give you power?" asked Sam.

"Virtual Reality is more advanced than anyone's ever realised. While you're using it, your very soul enters the game, not just a computerised version of yourself. Using that, I was able to trap his soul in the game, and stage some kind of death in the real world to get rid of his empty shell of a body. Then I took over his game body, using it to complete the game and lure more people here. Stealing their power, or, as it is called by most, Dragon Dust."

"What did you do to the real creator, and his dragon?"

"The creator's spirit is still here, unconscious, and never to awaken again. He didn't have a dragon, just a simple robot designed to act as his companion. So I changed it, got rid of all its feelings, and made it into the ultimate game character, the Destroyer. But that wasn't all he had created. That stupid Dragon Council, with all their power, managed to take some other players here. But they did come in handy, creating all those rules. So many restrictions that I can break, so many laws to protect me."

By now, Maree was feeling frightened. She was trapped, in a game, with some mad spirit of a creature too terrible to be allowed to live in the real world. But he didn't bring her here just to tell her that. He wanted to do something.

"What is it you want?" she asked.

"To cause as much pain and suffering as I can, and I know a good place to start. You know your friend Ceirin? He's my apprentice."

*   *   *

Izzy stood outside the doorway to the room, watching the girl cry. Emotions, what a waste of human ability. A weakness that every-one of those creatures possessed. When was she going to stop, and let him kill her? His master had ordered him to cause her pain, and her sadness was doing that. But it wasn't any fun if he wasn't causing it!

From behind fake tears, Ellen looked at the robot. That boy's words hadn't saddened her, but only made her more angry. Crystal knew Ellen had been as good a tamer as she could; all that he had said was lies.

And now he had set the Destroyer to attack her. It was strange. She knew it was a robot, but it seemed so human. It didn't seem fair, that robot having to take orders from such a monster. It was smart. Maybe, if she tried to talk to it...

She stood up, and it moved towards her at such a speed that before she could blink one blade was at her throat and another at her stomach.

"Please!" asked Ellen. "Wait! I don't want to fight you, I just want to talk!"

"Talk? There is no point, except to give commands."

"You don't have to do what you're commanded."

"Does not compute. Must obey commands." the robot said, pausing to think about the idea.

"Don't you ever want to be free?" she asked. It looked at her blankly.

"Searching database for 'Freedom'...No Data found..." it said.

"You don't know what freedom is?"

"Error! Must not interact. Must continue with mission."

"You don't have to. You can think for yourself."

"M-must obey. Must obtain amulet." One of its blades turned into a hand, and it grabbed for the amulet.

"You must have some feelings..." whispered Ellen as it pulled the chain tight around her throat, and the amulet glowed in Izzy's fist. The robot fell back, dragging Ellen with him. She gasped for breath, and the amulet loosened as it fell out of his grasp. The sudden release made her fall backwards, instead of towards the blades. She got up, panting for breath, and saw the robot jerking on the floor.

"D-does not c-c-compute. Freedom...feelings...original creation." it said. "A friend...friendship. A feeling. Error. Wh-what has happened? The boy…my friend…changing…change for both of us…memories…so many memories…"

"Are you alright?" asked Ellen as it got up

"Does not compute…why…why am I doing this…?" it asked.

"Well, because you were told to."

"But…but…original purpose…error…not true…friend…" it mumbled.

"Return to your master. He might be able to fix you." suggested Ellen, running off in the direction the boy had gone.

"Master…not true…not true master…Return to master…" it said, heading in the opposite direction to Ellen.

*   *   *

Ceirin's path had taken him to the computer room, where his master built robots and worked on the game. This was how he controlled everything, a network of computers, laptops, and PDA's.

"Master, I have done what you requested." shouted Ceirin, his voice echoing around the empty room.

"Good, now go down the stairs to your left. I'll meet you there," was the reply.

Ceirin felt uneasy. He hated going lower down, to the dungeons. Trap doors were everywhere, and iZ was always nearby.

"Hurry up, boy. Why should you be afraid of your master?"

"For plenty of reasons." said Nick under his breath, following in dog form, tail and eyes to the ground. Silently, Ceirin agreed.

The boy was standing against a wall, watching him as he came down. Not a good sign.

"Good job, boy." he said, knowing how much Ceirin hated being called a boy by someone barely a year older than he was.

"I have done as you requested." said Ceirin. He paused.

"Yes?" replied the Spirit, waiting for Ceirin to continue.

"Now may I make a request?" asked Ceirin.

"What is it? You should know better than to ask for something from me," sighed the boy.

"That you don't hurt my friends," demanded Ceirin.

"Ah…it is too late."

122

"Too late for what?" asked Nick sharply.

"For many things, now be quiet. I am talking to your tamer, not a formless creature like you."

"May I know why?" Ceirin asked nervously.

"For one, it's too late for your friends. Izzy is dealing with the girl without a dragon, and I shall soon deal with the other and her dragon. For another, it is too late for you."

"What do you mean?" demanded Nick.

"Silence!" Shouted the boy, kicking Nick against a wall with such force the stone cracked. "You have a weakness, both of you, that neither I nor iZ have. It makes you weak, and I cannot stand it."

"I have no weakness." Ceirin said firmly.

"Yes you do, you're a human. A pathetic human. And you have feelings. Feeling for your dragon, feelings for those girls, feelings about everything! You didn't want those girls to be hurt, nor your dragon. You're scared that I shall kill you. I expected more from you, but you are only human… I shouldn't have saved you in the first place."

"The kelpie…those Kilimario…those grey creatures…"

"All designed to kill you. All would have, but you had 'friends' to help you, the ability to overcome your fear, and those stupid thoughts about being a dragon tamer."

"How do you know what I was thinking?"

"I merely watched you talking to Nick. What you said while in Konica was enough to convince me. Poor scared Ceirin. Terrified of his own master. For good reason of course, for I no longer have any use for you," he said, and Ceirin froze as the boy ran his cold fingers along his neck and tore off the wave changer, crushing it in his hand.

"The castle is completely locked. No one goes in, no one goes out. Except me of course."

"You can't touch me without breaking the rules," hissed Ceirin.

"The rules, such feeble things," laughed the boy. "But I am the creator of this game; I can break them, bend them, twist and turn them however I want."

From beneath Ceirin's feet, the floor started to shake, and he jumped out of the way as it opened beneath him.

"I'd watch your step, if I were you. I took the liberty of putting the snake guardian down there, just in case."

"What are you going to do to me?"

"Me? Nothing. It is iZ who shall kill you. All I shall do is tell him to give you your reward, for being such a faithful player."

"What reward?"

"A quick death, of course."

"Why don't you just wipe my memory?"

"Memory wipes, such clever things. But the spell that causes them can be broken. And anyway, killing is much more fun." Grinned the boy. "iZ will execute you as soon as I have finished with the others. Have a nice day." With a laugh, he turned and walked away.

"No!" shouted Ceirin, moving after the boy.

"Tut, tut, tut. I'm not that stupid, you should know that by now." The boy teased as Ceirin received a jolt of electricity through his body. "Did I forget to mention my newest designs. Cages made from pure electricity. You can't see them, but you can feel them," he said, waving as he left the dungeon. "Goodbye!"

*   *   *

Ceirin stood there for a while, thinking about what was going to happen, though trying not to think about it. Nick was against the wall, surrounded by another of those cages. So he thought about the only other thing he could, his anger at the game. It had ruined his life. He couldn't even go home! And his stupid master had forced him to betray his only friends. He deserved this, after what he had done to them...

Nick, trapped in some strange cage he couldn't see, was worried for his tamer. Not only had he done something terrible to his two friends, sending them to their death, but he didn't seem in a good state of mind. He was finally being forced to deal with everything he had done, and Nick wasn't sure if he could cope with it. Nick was right. He couldn't.

An odd light came into his eyes. He had figured out a way to get rid of all these emotions. That girl, Maree, it was her fault. She had made him do it. If he had never met her, this wouldn't have happened. If he got rid of her, he would feel better.

His thoughts were interrupted by something entering the dungeon from above. The Destroyer.

Had his friends been killed already? It didn't look like it. The robot had his hands out instead of weapons. Surely he didn't...it was too horrible to think about.

Ceirin closed his eyes and waited. Was the robot enjoying taking his time?

He could hear Nick nearby, screaming and yelling as he shape-shifted randomly, trying to escape. The electricity was everywhere, there was no way he could escape and go help his tamer.

But the robot was acting strangely. His movements were jerky, his eyes kept scanning the room over and over.

"Not my m-m-master," it stuttered. "Cannot find master."

"Are you operating properly, iZ?" asked Ceirin, while trying hard to keep his balance and avoid falling through the trap door, below which the snake guardian was hissing expectantly.

"Error. Cannot remember commands," it said, louder than it normally did. Below, the snake guardian was, listening.

"You don't remember what you were told to do?" asked Ceirin, amazed at his luck.

"Command error. Data damaged. Recovering data..." it mumbled. Below, the snake guardian started speaking, shouting up at the robot.

"There isssssssss no need for that. I remember your commandssssssssssss." it shouted up.

"You have data?" asked the robot.

"Yesssssssssss. Do you ssssssssssee that boy? You mussssssssst throw him down the hole to me, he sssssssssaid."

"I must?"

"Stop the snake guardian, idiot!" Nick shouted at Ceirin, who was standing confused in the middle of everything.

"Izzy!" yelled Ceirin, finally realising what was going on. "You have to return to your master to get your real commands. I'll show you where he is," said Ceirin, turning to show the way and shocking himself on the cage. He lost his balance, but he had known that would happen, and manage to regain it.

"Why are you imprisoned?" Asked the robot.

"I…I trapped myself in here by accident. I was testing out the new cages. Can you help me?"

"Command received by master's apprentice. Clearance to obey received." it said, going over to the main computer and plugging himself in. "Searching… cage deactivated."

"Your master is up those stairs, Destroyer. You should be careful. A lot of your programming seems damaged. You're not meant to ask questions."

"I am sorry. Do you wish me to put you back in the cages and try again?"

"No! Just see if you can be fixed. And you're not meant to be polite, either."

"You really are an idiot, Ceirin," said Nick, brushing off dust from the stones. "Why didn't you tell him to go the wrong way?"

"Obviously, because he might have come back." Ceirin said, shrugging. "He'll come back anyway, as soon as he starts working again and is given his commands. Then he'll come looking for you using his proper speed."

"Well at least I tried! Are you O.K. after being kicked like that?"

"I'll be fine," said Nick, trying to avoid wincing from the pain in his chest. "I'll still be able to shape-shift. Now can we leave?"

"No. I have to go see Maree."

"She's probably dead," said Nick sadly.

"Not if Izzy's just gone up."

"Are you going to help her?"

"No. It's her fault this happened."

"It's not, you know it isn't!" yelled Nick angrily.

"I am your tamer, and you will do what I command." Ceirin said sharply.

"No wonder he chose you as his apprentice. You're just like him," growled Nick.

"No, I have feelings. And I'm feeling angry," said Ceirin, with a grin too similar to the creator's.

126

Chapter 21: *Sacrifice*

Once the creator had left, Maree and Sam had been left in the huge room, to try and make sense of what had just happened. Ceirin couldn't have betrayed them, could he? Then, the boy had returned, and soon after him came iZ, then Ceirin.

"That's it! I've had enough! This whole game had ruined my life! So now, I'm going to ruin yours!" Ceirin cried when he reached the top. Sam and Maree were there, talking to his controller.

"What are you doing here?" the boy exclaimed as Ceirin came in.

"Shut up." Ceirin said sharply. Nick flew past him in eagle form, and changed into a rope, dragging Izzy and the boy together, and then changed once more to form a metal cage. He knew Ceirin wouldn't want the two to interfere.

Ceirin darted forward, and grabbed Sam by the neck, pulling her against him.

"What are you doing?!" asked Maree. Surly that couldn't be Ceirin? His smile, his eyes, he had become like the creator, an evil being.

He had his hand around Sam's neck and, as she struggled and lashed out with her claws and tail, he drew out a harmonica, and flicked it twice through the air. It changed into a small blade, which he pressed against Sam's throat. She immediately stopped struggling, and froze, not even daring to breathe. The knife was small, but sharp enough to slit her throat in seconds.

"You wouldn't dare..." said Maree, but the look in Ceirin's eyes told her that he would. She drew her sword.

"Don't even try it. She'd be dead before it reached me." Ceirin said, pressing the blade into Sam's neck. The dragon gasped, the movement making it cut even deeper.

Maree raised the sword, looking at Ceirin. He tensed, pressing the knife in further. But instead of attacking Ceirin, she slowly slid it down her own arm. Red blood oozed out, staining the sword. Ceirin gasped, watching her.

"This is a game. You're not supposed to bleed!" Cried Ceirin, shocked.

"It's more than a game. Lift the blade," said Maree. It was a command, not a request.

Still shocked, Ceirin raised the blade, and saw red blood also flowing from the cut on the Dragon's neck. The blade fell to the floor.

"Haven't you realised it yet, Ceirin?" Maree said sadly. "Even after all you've been through. It's more than just a game! We can be hurt, we can bleed! We can feel pain, and so can our dragons! It's real!"

"It's more than a game…" Ceirin sighed. Then he stopped, the gleam not leaving his eyes. "We can feel pain. We can die." He said, reaching down to pick up the blade. "This is my fault, all of it…And I shall pay for my mistakes with my life."

"No you won't," said Sam, and Ceirin had barely enough time to get his hand out of the way before she brought down her tail and crushed the knife into pieces.

Nick released the Creator and ran over in his Labrador form, lying next to a shaking Ceirin. "Thank you…" he whispered to Sam. Released, the boy turned on Ceirin.

"You escaped, then. Surprising, and improbable. But you did, unfortunately. However, I shall deal with you later, and this time I'll watch you die. And you will not be receiving your reward."

"You'd kill your own apprentice?" gasped Maree.

"Of course. I have no use for him now. Did you know that he tried to spare your lives? And by doing so, developing feelings and friendships, he shall be killed."

"You monster!"

"Thank you. I do enjoy a complement," sneered the boy.

" No wonder Ceirin acted like that. It's your fault. Crystal, Ceirin, everything. And I won't let you continue. I'll destroy you and your dragon!" yelled Maree.

Sam fired some bolts of lightning and jets of water, at Izzy, who was now able to move since Nick had released it's controller.

"You think that hurts?" laughed the evil spirit. "Not a bit. Izzy shares my energy; it cannot be defeated as long as I am safe."

"Then we'll fight you instead!" Maree said, still holding her sword.

"I wouldn't do that," he sneered, holding up the rulebook. "You can't touch me without getting a Game Over."

No wonder this level was unbeatable! You couldn't hurt that creature without losing the game! There had to be a way round this...She needed more time to think about it. But what could distract him?

"Hi everyone! Has that robot been fixed yet?" said Ellen, stepping into the arena. A grin was fixed on her face, hiding her anger.

"No...you should have been killed! Why didn't you do your job, iZ?" Demanded the boy.

"Error. Data corrupted. Commands unknown," replied Izzy.

"Perhaps I do need an apprentice after all..." muttered the boy. "Maybe I'll spare Ceirin..."

"I'd rather face the Snake Guardian that become a snake like it," growled Ceirin in response.

"Now, if nobody minds..." Ellen said, coughing politely. "I' m really angry, and I'm going to take it out on this creep, whatever the rules say."

"Oh great..."said the boy. You would think, with him having taken over the body of a genius that he could have thought up something better to say, but he didn't have time. Within seconds, Ellen was upon him, screaming like a wild beast.

"Get off me! You're not supposed to do that! It's against the rules!" he shouted, at the same time trying to fend Ellen off.

"Rules are meant to be broken!" she shouted, punching him in the face.

The spirit started twitching, then shaking, trying desperately to get away from Ellen. But she kept up her attack.

Everyone else stared at them. Ellen was behaving like an animal! They'd never seen her act like this before, and now they were, it was alarming. As she punched and kicked the boy, the robot seemed in pain. Its movements were slowing, its strength failing. Ellen caught sight of it, and stopped.

"This isn't right. He shouldn't have to die because of you."

"If I die, he dies. You'll have to let us both live," the Creator said, grinning.

Pinning the boy down, Ellen stared at the robot, then back at the boy.

129

"No. I'll rebuild him; make him better than what you made him. Then all your evil will have left him."

"So you're just going to kill him?" said the creator, panic in his voice.

"No. I won't kill you. I'll let the robot who's having to die because of you do that."

Izzy had slowed to a stop, and was standing rigid, staring at his master. *His beloved creator, who had changed and made this happen. He was in such pain because of him. He had been created as companion, a friend, and even though he had been changed into a simple fighting machine, his loyalty to his master hadn't changed. Even he could tell this wasn't the boy who had made him. He would help save his original creator, even if it meant sacrificing himself.* He raised his gun to his chest… and fired.

"No! This can't be happeniiiiiiiiiiiiiiiiiing!" cried the Spirit, as a dark shape lifted out of the body, and rushed out of the fort and into the fog, which soon after disappeared.

As every part of his body shut down, iZ managed to catch a glimpse of what was happening, and see his true master return, before his eyes faded to grey and he shut down completely, a grin appearing on his face. The first time he'd grinned in a year, and the last time D-1 iZ ever would.

Ellen stood up, and the Creator rose, shaking his head and looking dazed. Ceirin asked if he was feeling better.

"Better…" he said, sighing. "…Thank you."

"My name's Ellen."

"I…" He paused, remembering something. "I am the Creator."

"Maree," said Ceirin, "I'm so sorry…"

"I forgive you. It wasn't your fault, he was controlling you. Let's forget the past."

"I only wish Ellen could…" sighed Ceirin.

"At least she seems to have found a friend…" Sam said, as Maree walked over to the pair.

"So, can we go home now?" asked Maree.

"I'm afraid it's not that simple," replied the Creator." You're stuck inside the game."

Chapter 22 : *The Truth Revealed*

"You mean…we can't go home….." said Maree, shaking.

"No. In the real world, you're dead. It is only here, in the game, that you are alive," said The Creator.

"We really did die?" asked Maree, shocked.

"Yes, you died when you drowned, Ceirin when he, like me, was murdered by the Spirit's minions"

"What happened to my body?" asked Ceirin.

"So that none of them could be examined, all of our empty bodies were moved to a different world by some of the spirit's minions."

"There's no way we can return to our original bodies…." said Ceirin.

"No, we cannot change the past, nor can we defeat Death," sighed the Creator.

Maree started sobbing. Ceirin tried to be optimistic, but it was hard.

"Hey, come on Maree, it's not that bad. We can create a world here, just like Earth, and live there…"

"I guess I'm trapped too…" murmured Ellen.

"Horse riding accident," said the creator quietly.

"The eyes?" Ellen asked.

"I'm not sure. I don't think the spirit planned for you to come, but his minions may still have had something to do with it."

"So…I can't get a game over, even if I have lost my Dragon. Can't she be reborn?" said Ellen, and as she said this, tears formed in her eyes, thinking about Crystal.

"I could try and retrieve her data, but I don't think I can. I could, however, create a new one for you. It could look exactly like her."

"It wouldn't be the same."

"Then you can create a new one," suggested Ceirin.

"No. I'm not ready to forget," said Ellen, walking off into the shadows. Her one hope, the thought that had kept her going through all the battles, all the side quests, all of the game, had gone. She had nothing now.

"She looked so sad." said Ceirin, after she had left.

"She has no one now. She can't return home to her family, she has no Dragon to keep her company, she's heart broken," said Maree sadly.

"There's nothing we can do to help her. We have to get on with our own lives, in the game," said Ceirin.

"You're right. If we're going to be stuck in this world, why not make it the best world to be stuck in?" said Maree, smiling.

Feeling out of place, the Creator stepped away, letting them talk in peace.

"But there's something bothering me..." said Ceirin. "Ever since we defeated that spirit, I've felt like something's missing. Something happened, but I don't know what is. All I can remember is working for the spirit, but I'm sure that can't be it all. This game hasn't existed that long, I should have some other memories. I can't remember being younger, I can't even remember my old life on Earth."

"I don't want to remember my past..." said Maree.

"Why not?"

"Something happened a long time ago. I keep trying to forget about it but I can't. Once, I was best friends with this other player. He went to fight the destroyer, but I wouldn't follow because I was terrified Sam would get hurt. He kept asking me to come, and I got angry and said that if he wanted to go and get himself killed, then it was fine with me, and he left. I never saw him again. I looked up his player information and it said he had been defeated." As she finished, both Ceirin and Nick gave a cry and fell to the floor. Sam and Maree watched in horror as they writhed in pain.

"Ceirin? Nick? What's wrong?" shouted Sam. Ceirin's eyes were rolling, while Nick was shape-shifting so fast his body was a blur. During this, the creator came back and explained what was happening.

"It's one of those spirits spells. They're trying to break its power!"

"It's what's stopping him remember. That spirit must have done something to him when Ceirin became his apprentice," said Sam. "Like a memory block!"

"You have to get them to calm down. If this keeps on, they could badly hurt themselves," the Creator said calmly.

"Ceirin, Nick, we know what you're trying to do. You have to try hard and break its power! We've defeated the Destroyer, we've defeated sphinxes and you have to be able to do this. You need to try and calm down, and try to remember." Maree said soothingly.

Sam tried a different approach. She blasted the two with a jet of water. Neither seemed to help.

Behind them stood Ellen, silently watching everything as she thought over what had happened. She'd have to return to Fear Fork soon. She needed to be with Crystal.

But now this was happening.

Almost everybody seemed to want that strange amulet Crystal had left, so it had to have some sort of power. Maybe she could use it against the magic that was doing this to her friends. "Help them, Crystal," she murmured. As if in response, the amulet glowed, and Ceirin and Nick stopped moving and sat still, dazed.

"Maree. I...I think I finally remember what happened. A long time ago, I was a normal player. In the real world, I was sitting playing my laptop on the bank of my local canal. In the game, I went to fight the destroyer, but the Snake Guardian defeated me. I thought I would return to reality, but something stopped me, as though I wasn't allowed back. Then the creator came to me and offered to let me back into the game, but I would have to work as his apprentice."

"I remember that too. Most of the time, I was unconscious in my own mind while that wretched spirit used my body, but sometimes I woke up. I remember hearing the spirit talking with the Destroyer. The robot said another player had died in the real world while playing, and was going to re-enter the game. The creator said it was the perfect chance for him to gain a spy. He said he would go and see the player before he was returned to the game automatically, and offer him a chance to keep on playing. He

133

would erase the players memory, and fool the Dragon Council into thinking they had brought him there to fight him. Then he would use the player to spy on the others brought to the game and stop them reaching him."

"They tricked him!" said Sam. "He would have returned to the game either way!"

"I remember that too. I was confused, and decided to become a shape-shifter to match my Tamer's ever changing personality. So this isn't my true form!"

A bright flash of light filled the room, blinding everyone. When it faded, the Destroyer's apprentice had gone, and in his place stood Ceirin, the Ceirin Maree had once known. And in the shape-shifter's place stood the true Nick. A white, winged wolf, with silver eyes that glinted in the light, an Air Dragon. Able to control the flow of air, causing hurricanes, tornadoes, gales, or even calming any of these down, he could also communicate with creatures of the air.

"Air..." said Sam. "Not a bad element..."

The Truth had finally been revealed...

Chapter 23 : *Offline*

That day, the game was offline for twelve hours. After all, how could the Dragon Tamer's have a party if players kept walking in? It was the biggest celebration the game world had ever seen. Everyone who had taken part in their adventure came, the imp, the Sphinxes, Kilimario (the nice ones), squirrels, the sirens, who had to stay outside in a swimming pool and spent most of the time trying to ask the creator to stop the sun from destroying them (who replied that it never *actually* was going to collide, and was put there to make the planet more exciting, to the siren's anger), some kitecats (mostly small ones), some falcons (who most of the people stayed out of sight of, just in case), the kelpie (who stayed in the pool and fought with the sirens), some of the grey ghost things (which Ceirin hid from each time he saw them), some squirrels (who were checked for nuts before entering, but managed to get their hands on some during the meal), and almost every other creature in the whole of Dragon Tamers. There were a few fights, and there wasn't a lot of room, but no one had ever had more fun.

The Creator had let them use Destro Castle for the party, but wasn't there long. He kept disappearing to one of the many workshops in the castle, or going out for rides on his motorbike.

After the party, as the tamers tried to recover, they realised something. Ellen had disappeared. Again.

*   *   *

Ellen kept walking, far away from the rest of the humans, until she reached the spot where the web had been, and where she had found those strange items. It was nothing more than a clearing now, empty. But someone else was there.

"Who are you?" she asked, looking at the figure in the trees. "What are you doing here?"

135

"It is not important. But I know who you are, Ellen. And I can help you."

"I don't need help," said Ellen.

"You miss your dragon, don't you? That's why you come here."

"You can't help with that."

"On the contrary, friend. I *can* help you. I can bring back your Dragon, I can return you to Earth, and I can do anything your heart desires."

"What do I have to do?" questioned Ellen.

"Simple. I need your help...and your amulet..."